George Washington Moon

Bad English Exposed

A series of criticisms on the errors and inconsistencies of Lindley Murray and other

grammarians

George Washington Moon

Bad English Exposed
A series of criticisms on the errors and inconsistencies of Lindley Murray and other grammarians

ISBN/EAN: 9783337410223

Printed in Europe, USA, Canada, Australia, Japan

Cover: Foto ©Andreas Hilbeck / pixelio.de

More available books at **www.hansebooks.com**

BAD ENGLISH EXPOSED:

A SERIES OF CRITICISMS

ON THE ERRORS AND INCONSISTENCIES OF

Lindley Murray and other Grammarians.

BY

G. WASHINGTON MOON,

MEMBER OF THE COUNCIL

OF THE ROYAL SOCIETY OF LITERATURE,

AUTHOR OF

"THE DEAN'S ENGLISH", ETC.

Fourth Edition.

———

" The rules of our language should breathe the same spirit as the laws
"of our country. They should be bars against licentiousness, without
" being checks to liberty."—*Campbell's* ' *Philosophy of Rhetoric.*'

LONDON:

HATCHARDS, PICCADILLY.

1871.

PREFACE.

My former work, "*The Dean's English*", to which this is the companion volume, is a series of criticisms on the language employed by the Dean of Canterbury in his treatise on the Queen's English and demonstrates that while the Dean undertook to instruct others he was himself but a castaway in matters of grammar.

The present work is a similar series of criticisms, but is on the English of certain Americans; namely, Lindley Murray, the Hon. G. P. Marsh, Mr. S. of Trinity College, and Mr. E. S. Gould of New York.

Lindley Murray was born at Swatara in Pennsylvania. He studied law and practised at the bar until the breaking out of the war of independence, when he became a merchant, and soon amassed a handsome fortune which enabled him to retire. The remaining years of his life were spent in England; here he wrote his celebrated *"English Grammar"*, and other works, and died in February, 1826.

The Hon. G. P. Marsh is a native of Vermont, U. S. A. After occupying several important offices in that State, he became a member of the Federal Congress, subsequently United States' Minister at Constantinople, and is now United States' Minister at Florence. But his real distinction is as a scholar; and especially as a linguist. He is a rival of Bowring as a polyglot, and has attained deserved eminence as a master both of Northern and of Oriental languages.

Mr. S., who defends certain of Mr. Marsh's expressions, is one of the professors in Trinity College, Hartford.

Mr. E. S. Gould is a son of the late Hon. Judge Gould of Connecticut, who was one of the most eminent jurists, graceful speakers, and accomplished scholars in the United States. Judge Gould was also especially distinguished for purity and precision as a writer of English. Mr. E. S. Gould has therefore a sort of hereditary claim to rank as a purist in English style; and he has long been recognised in America as an authority in matters of literary and philological criticism.

12 COLLEGE TERRACE,
 BELSIZE PARK,
  LONDON, N.W.

CONTENTS.

———

ARTICLES.

" The structure of language is extremely artificial; and there
" are few sciences in which a deeper or more refined logic is
" employed, than in grammar.   It is apt to be slighted by
" superficial thinkers, as belonging to those rudiments of know-
" ledge, which were inculcated upon us in our earliest youth.
" But what was then inculcated before we could comprehend its
" principles, would abundantly repay our study in maturer
" years."

DR. HUGH BLAIR'S
'Lectures on Rhetoric and Belles Lettres.'

BAD ENGLISH EXPOSED.

CRITICISM I.

LINDLEY MURRAY.

OF all the tasks of our school days, perhaps none
was more repugnant to any of us, than the
study of grammar; and when, after many a good
caning, we had at last, in some fashion, mastered
its rules, our estimate of their value was not very
different from the charity boy's estimate of the
value of the alphabet which he had just learnt;
—we questioned whether it was worth while going
through so much to learn so little.

The task of working out a puzzling sum in
arithmetic, or of solving a difficult problem in
geometry, was, to say the least of it, one possess-
ing some degree of interest; but what interest
could attach to the studying of rules concerning
verbs and pronouns? The determining of the

B

cost of a horse by the progressive amounts to be
paid for the nails in his shoes, or the feat of
crossing the famous bridge in the first book of
Euclid, was, to most of us, a matter of pride;
but what pride could a boy take in learning that
" a verb is a word which signifies ' to be ', ' to do ',
" or ' to suffer ' " ?

' To suffer ' ! I can imagine the almost mali-
cious pleasure which Lindley Murray felt as he
wrote those words, and thought of the prophetic
significance which they had for the luckless urchins
who should fail to understand his rules of grammar.   Well, it is the pupil's turn now; and,
notwithstanding that the old grammarian was a
personal friend of my family's, I cannot resist
the temptation to take up the pen against him,
and to repay him for the terror of his name in
my school days, by showing that, in the very
volume in which he laid down his rules, he
frequently expressed himself ungrammatically.

However, it is not merely to gratify, even good
humouredly, a boyish feeling of retaliation, that
I enter upon this task.   My chief object is to
render some little service to those who are
desirous of acquiring a critical knowledge of the
English language, but who are in danger of being

misled in their studies, by the bad English of one
who has been considered our principal grammarian.

I will not criticise the first edition of his work;
nor, indeed, any one of the seventy editions
which, including abridgments, were issued before
the work had received the author's final emendations; but will, in simple justice to him, confine
my criticisms to the most accurate edition published—the two volume octavo edition of 1816,
which he describes, both on the title page and
in the preface, as "*corrected*".

First, then, he says, in strangely ungrammatical language, on page 10;—

"From the sentiment generally admitted, that a
" proper selection of faulty composition is more
" instructive to the young grammarian, than [are]
" any rules and examples of propriety that can be
" given, the compiler has been induced to pay
" particular attention to this part of the subject;
" and though the instances of false grammar,
" under the rules of syntax, are numerous, it is
" hoped [that] they will not be found too many,
" when their variety and usefulness are con-
" sidered."

I, also, hope that the following instances of
false grammar, taken from Lindley Murray's own

composition, will not be found too many, when their variety and usefulness are considered ;— their "variety", because they relate to almost every part of speech in the language ; and their "usefulness ", because such errors, when pointed out as having been committed by one who professes to be a master of composition, are more impressive, and therefore more instructive, than any number of examples of good English could possibly be.

It is scarcely necessary to mention that, in the foregoing quotation, Lindley Murray really says ;—" A proper selection of faulty composition "*is* more instructive than [is] any rules and " examples "!

A similar error occurs on page 365 ; there he says ;—

> " Many sentences *are* miserably mangled, and the
> " force of the emphasis [*are*] totally lost ".

Here, also, the ellipsis of the second verb is unallowable ; because, as in the former instance, the number of the nominative to that verb, is not the same as the number of the nominative to the preceding verb.   In the one instance there is a change from the singular to the plural; in

the other, a change from the plural to the
singular; and, in any such sentence, either of
those changes will make it imperative that the
second verb be expressed. The latter passage
should have been written thus :—" Many sen-
"tences *are* miserably mangled, and the force of
" the emphasis *is* totally lost ".

Again, on page 497, I read as follows :—

> " Where a riddle is not intended, it is always a fault
> " in allegory to be too dark. [A mere truism!
> " Of course it is a fault to be *too* dark.] The
> " meaning should be easily seen, through the
> " figure employed to shadow it. However, the
> " proper mixture of light and shade, in such
> " compositions : the exact adjustment of all the
> " figurative circumstances with the literal sense,
> " so as neither to lay the meaning too bare and
> " open, nor to cover and wrap it up too much;
> " have [has] ever been considered as points [a
> " point] of great nicety ".

If the reader will carefully examine this passage, he will see that the nominative to the verb,
"*considered*", is in the singular number; and
therefore the verb should have been in the
singular; for, as Lindley Murray himself tells
us, on page 218 ;—"A verb must agree with its
" nominative case, in number and person ".   The
nominative is, " *the proper mixture of light and*

"*shade ;* what follows is merely a repetition, or an enlargement, of that idea ; as may be shown in a very few words. Thus, "*the exact adjust-* "*ment*", mentioned in the latter part of the sentence, is but an other name for "*the proper* "*mixture*", spoken of in the early part : "*to lay* "*the meaning too bare and open*" is an illustration of the term "*light*"; and, "*to cover and* "*wrap it up too much*" is an amplification of the thought conveyed by the term "*shade*". Lindley Murray ought therefore to have said ;—"The "proper mixture of light and shade......*has* ever "been considered a point of great nicety". He has here violated the first rule of syntax !

The misuse of the adverb "*too*", at which I glanced in a previous paragraph, is very common. It occurs several times, even in ' *Murray's* ' *Grammar.*' We find it on pages 465, 474, 476, and 497. The last of these passages, I have already quoted; the others run thus :—

"They should not be *too* frequently repeated".
" We should not do well to introduce such hard and " strong sounds *too* frequently ".
"The members of a sentence......should not be *too* "long ".

Comment upon this point is needless.

An other very common error,—the using of a wrong tense of the verb " *to be* ",—occurs on page 367 ; there he says ;—

"As the communication of these internal feelings,
" *was* of much more consequence in our social
" intercourse, than the mere conveyance of ideas,
" the Author of our being did not, as in that
" conveyance, leave the invention of the language
" of emotion, to man; but impressed it Himself
" upon our nature ".

Had Lindley Murray been speaking, not of a universal truth, but of a circumstance that was peculiar to the past, his sentence would have been correct ; but he himself says, on page 283 ; —" In referring to declarations of this nature, "the present tense must be used, *if the position* " *is immutably the same at all times, or supposed* " *to be so :* as, ' The bishop declared, that virtue " ' *is* always advantageous ' : not, ' *was* always " ' advantageous ' ". According to Lindley Murray's own showing, then, he ought to have said ;— " As the communication of these internal feelings " *is* of much more consequence in our social "intercourse ", etc.

Some persons, intending to be strictly accurate in their expressions, always say ;—" *if it be* ",

"*though it were*"; never, "*if it is*", "*though it*
"*was*". They imagine that "*if*", "*though*",
and certain other conjunctions which imply contingency, ought always to be followed by a verb
in the subjunctive mood. But it is only when
there is *a concurrence of contingency and futurity*,
that the verb should be in the subjunctive mood.
When there is either contingency without futurity,
or futurity without contingency, the verb must be
in the indicative mood. The only exception to
this rule occurs in the use of the imperfect tense
of the verb "*to be*," when our language is intended to denote contingency merely. The verb
must then be in the subjunctive mood. See
Lindley Murray's observations on Rule XIX of
his '*Grammar*.' But, notice how widely his
practice diverges from his precepts :—

> Page 51.—" A consonant is not of itself a distinct
> " articulate voice; and its influence in varying the
> " tones of language *is* not clearly perceived, unless
> " it be [is] accompanied by an opening of the
> " mouth, that is, by a vowel."

> Page 64.—"If this be [is] admitted, it *follows*, that
> " the noun and the verb *are* the only parts of
> " speech, which are essentially necessary."

> Page 193.—" When a discourse *is* not well connected,
> " the sentiments, however just, *are* easily for-

" gotten; or, if a few be [are] remembered, yet
" their general scope and tendency, having never
" been clearly apprehended, *is* [are] not remem-
" bered at all."

The reader will perceive, by the italicised words
in the foregoing quotations, that in each instance
the time of the action is *present*, not *future*.
Therefore, the verb which follows the conjunction
ought to be in the indicative mood.

The last of the passages quoted contains two
errors; for, Lindley Murray errs not only in
employing the subjunctive mood, but also in
putting in the singular number, a verb, to which
the nominative is in the plural. Thus he violates
his second rule of syntax, which says;—" Two
" or more nouns, etc. in the singular number,
" joined together by a copulative conjunction,
" expressed or understood, must have verbs,
" nouns, and pronouns, agreeing with them in
" the plural number".—Page 225.

Again, " It is evidently contrary to the first
" principles of grammar, to consider two distinct
" ideas as one, however nice may be their shades
" of difference: and if there be no difference,
" one of them must be superfluous, and ought to
" be rejected."—Page 226.

Dr. Blair, also, whom Lindley Murray quotes, observes that, "two or more substantives, joined "by a copulative, must *always* require the verb "or [the] pronoun to which they refer, to be "placed in the plural number." Lindley Murray adds, on page 227 ;—"and this is the general sen- "timent of English grammarians." Yet, he himself says, in the quotation which I have given ;—"their scope *and* tendency *is* [they is !] "not remembered at all."

These errors occur in the best edition of '*Lindley Murray's Grammar*'; an edition pub- lished under the supervision of the author ; and after his work had been one-and-twenty years before the public !

CRITICISM II.

LINDLEY MURRAY.

F⅃OM the consideration of Lindley Murray's errors in the use of verbs, let us now turn to that of his errors in the use of adverbs. He says, on page 290;—"Adverbs, though they have no government " of case, tense, etc. require an appropriate situa- " tion in the sentence ". Undoubtedly they do; and that situation, as we learn from page 445, is, as near as possible to the words which are most closely related to them. But has Lindley Murray uniformly placed his adverbs in appro- priate situations ? Certainly not. I read as follows :—

> Page 236.—"A term which *only implies* the idea of " persons ".

This should have been ;—" A term which im- " plies the idea of *persons only* ".

> Page 365.—" When the voice is *only suspended* for a " moment ".

This should have been;—"When the voice is "suspended for *only a moment*".

Sometimes the adverb is required to be placed after the auxiliary, and sometimes before it; and which of these constructions we should employ in a particular instance, will depend upon the meaning which we wish to express. For example; if we wish to say that it is proper that certain rules should be written; our words may be arranged thus :—"The rules should *properly be* "written". But if we wish to say, not that it is proper that they should be written; but, that they should be written in a proper manner; then we must change the position of the adverb and say;—"The rules should *be properly* written". This is very simple; but it is a matter which has been quite overlooked by Lindley Murray, as the following passages will show :—

> Page 102.—"Perhaps the words 'former' and 'latter'
> " may *be properly* ranked amongst the demonstra-
> " tive pronouns ".

Say, rather ;—" may *properly be* ranked".

> Page 300.—"The preposition 'among' . . . .
> " cannot *be properly* used in conjunction with the
> " word 'every'".

Say, rather ;—" cannot *properly be* used".

Page 403.—" The colon may *be properly* applied in the
" three following cases."

" Say, rather ;—" may *properly be* applied ".

In the foregoing sentences, Lindley Murray
speaks of the things as being *properly done;*
whereas, he intended to speak of them as being
proper to do. See some remarks on this subject in
· *The Dean's English*', page 101.

The adverb *"also"* is misplaced by Lindley
Murray ; *e.g.* :—

Page 415.—" The first word of an example may *also*
" *very properly* begin with a capital ".

Better thus :—" The first word of *an example*
" *also,* may very properly begin ", etc.

The adverbs, " *rather* " and " *even* ", likewise,
are misplaced by him. Indeed, the former is
misplaced in a sentence occurring in the very
part of his *Grammar,* which treats of the proper
position of adverbs !

Page 293.—" This mode of expression *rather suits*
" familiar than grave style."

Our grammarian should have said ;—" suits a
" familiar *rather than* a grave style."

Page 454.—" It is a frequent and capital error, in *the*
" *writings even* of some distinguished authors ".

This should have been;—"in the writings of
"*even some distinguished* authors".

Concerning such sentences as those which I
have quoted, and the position of adverbs generally, Dr. Blair says;—"The fact is, with respect
"to such adverbs as, *only, wholly, at least,* and
"the rest of that tribe, that in common discourse,
"the tone and emphasis we use in pronouncing
"them, generally serves [*they serves!*] to show
"their reference, and to make the meaning clear;
"and hence, we acquire a habit of throwing them
"in loosely in the course of a period.   But, in
"writing, where a man speaks to the eye and
"not to the ear, he ought to be more accurate;
"and so to connect those adverbs with the words
"which they qualify, as to put his meaning out
"of doubt upon the first inspection."—'*Lectures
'on Rhetoric*', page 116.

There is one other matter of which I must
speak before concluding my remarks on adverbs; and that is, the misuse of what may be
called superlative adverbs; such as "*totally*",
"*supremely*", "*absolutely*", and "*universally*".
The nature of these words forbids their being
qualified by "*so*", or "*more*", or "*most*"; or
indeed, by any word implying comparison.   The

reason is obvious.   Take, for example, the adverb
"*totally*".   It is evident that if we attempt to
qualify it by prefixing the word "*so*", we convey
the idea that there are degrees of totality; in
other words, that a thing may, for instance, be
totally unknown, and yet not totally unknown.
In short, our expression amounts to the absurdity
of saying, that a whole may be either less or
more than itself!

On page 250, Lindley Murray very justly objects
to the expressions "*so* extreme", "*so* universal",
"etc.; because, adjectives that have in themselves a superlative signification, do not admit
of either the superlative or the comparative
form super-added.   But, surely, what is, in this
respect, true of superlative adjectives, is true
equally of the corresponding adverbs?   Yet we
should scarcely learn this from Lindley Murray's
own language; for, on page 501, he speaks of
certain objects as being

"*So totally* unknown"!

Respecting adverbs and adjectives, it has been
remarked that it is often difficult to decide, in
particular sentences, whether an adverb, or an

adjective ought to be used. For example, on
page 287, Lindley Murray says;—

"This construction sounds rather harshly".

Is this sentence correct? I think not. The
verb *"sounds"*, as there used, is a neuter verb;
one not expressing an action, but a state of
being; and neuter verbs should not be qualified
by adverbs, but by adjectives.

This is in accordance with Lindley Murray's
own teaching.   He tells us, on page 163, of vol. 2,
that, in such cases, we ought to consider whether
we wish to express *quality*, or *manner*. If quality,
then we must employ an adjective; if manner,
then, an adverb.   In the foregoing quotation, as
he did not wish to speak of the *manner of
sounding*, but of the *quality of sound*, he ought
to have said ;—" The construction sounds rather
" harsh" ; not *" harshly"*.

The following examples, taken from '*Lindley
'Murray's Grammar*', illustrate this matter very
forcibly :—

" She looks *cold*."—" She looks *coldly* on him."
" He feels *warm*."—" He feels *warmly* the insult offered
    "to him."

The reader will observe that when the verb is *intransitive*, *i.e.*, when the action does not pass on to some object, the *adjective* is used; *e.g.*: —" She looks *cold.*" But when the same verb is *transitive*, the *adverb* is used; *e.g.*:—" She looks " *coldly* on him."

An other mode of determining whether an adverb, or an adjective, should be employed, is thus given by Lindley Murray :—" The verb *to be*, " in all its moods and tenses, generally requires " the word immediately connected with it to be an " adjective, not an adverb ; and, consequently, " when this verb can be substituted for any other, " without varying the sense or the construction, " that other verb must also be connected with an " adjective. The following sentences elucidate " these observations :—' The rose smells [or *is*] " ' *sweet*'. ' How *delightful* the country appears ' " [or *is*]. ' The clouds look [or *are*] dark'. In " all these sentences, we can, with perfect pro- " priety, substitute some tenses of the verb *to be* " for the other verbs. But in the following " sentences, we cannot do this : " The dog smells " ' disagreeably'; ' George feels exquisitely'."

This is an excellent rule of Lindley Murray's ; but nothing could be more unfortunate than one of

his illustrations of it.   He very properly tells us
that we ought to say ;—" The rose smells *sweet* "
[is sweet] ; but he adds, or, at least, implies,
that we cannot say ;—" The dog smells disagree-
" able " [is disagreeable].   In other words, we
must say that, the scent of the rose is *sweet ;* but,
the scent of the dog is disagreea*bly !*

That such errors as these are to be found in
' *An English Grammar, Comprehending the Prin-*
' *ciples and Rules of the Language* ', is indeed
astonishing.

CRITICISM III.

LINDLEY MURRAY.

HAVING considered some of Lindley Murray's errors in the use of verbs, adverbs, and adjectives ; we will now consider some of his errors in the use of pronouns.

Concerning them, he says, on page 232;—"Pro-"nouns must always agree with their antecedents, "and the nouns for which they stand, in gender "and number". He adds, "Of this rule there "are many violations to be met with; a few of "which may be sufficient to put the learner on "his guard. '*Each* of the sexes should keep "'within *its* particular bounds, and content *them-*"'*selves* with the advantages of *their* particular "'districts'."

Although Lindley Murray thus endeavours "to "put the *learner* on his guard", the *teacher* so far forgets his own instructions, as to say, on page 416;—

c 2

"The facts, premises, and conclusions, of a subject,
"sometimes naturally point out the separations
"into paragraphs: and *each* of these, when of
"great length, will again require subdivision at
"*their* most distinctive parts." !

This is one of the most frequent of vulgar
errors.

An other, almost equally common, is the "*and*
"*which*" error. This consists in the employment
of the words "*and which*" in a sentence not
containing, in the preceding part of it, the word
"*which*", either expressed or understood. The
error is one that young writers frequently fall
into; and, strange to say, it is found in some of
even Lindley Murray's sentences. The following
example is from page 8 of his *Grammar :—*

"The more important rules, definitions, and observa-
"tions, *and which* are therefore the most proper
"to be committed to memory, are printed with a
"larger type".

This sentence is extremely faulty. Firstly, because it contains the "*and which*" error; and, secondly, because the relative adverb "*therefore*", that
follows those words, has really not any antecedent
that is grammatically connected with it. Lindley
Murray ought to have said;—"The rules, definitions,

" and observations *which are the more important,*
" *and which are therefore* the most proper to be com-
" mitted to memory, are printed in larger type".

The "*and which*" error occurs on page 379
also.   We there read :—

> "From the preceding view of English versification,
> " we may see what a copious stock of materials
> " it possesses.   For we are not only allowed the
> " use of all the ancient poetic feet, in our heroic
> " measure, but we have, as before observed, du-
> " plicates of each, agreeing in movement, though
> " differing in measure, *and which* make different
> " impressions on the ear; an opulence peculiar to
> " our language, *and which* may be the source of
> " a boundless variety."

Even were the foregoing sentence grammatically correct, the repetition of "*and which*"
would stamp it as being inelegant.   But the
sentence is constructed in direct violation of the
writer's eighteenth rule of syntax, which says ;—
" Conjunctions connect the same moods and
" tenses of verbs, and cases of nouns and pro-
" nouns ".   The latter part of the sentence
ought therefore to have been written thus :—
" But we have, as before observed, duplicates of
" each, *agreeing* in movement, though *differing*
" in measure, *and making* [not '*and which make*'

"different impressions on the ear; an opulence
"*which is* peculiar to our language, *and which*
"may be the source of a boundless variety."

The excessive employment of the pronoun
"*which*" is an error so common with the il-
literate, that good writers, in their endeavours to
avoid it, often run into the opposite extreme.
They omit the pronoun, in sentences where its
presence is really necessary to the grammatical
arrangement of the words. An instance of this
occurs in Lindley Murray's work, page 305. He
there says;—

"Almost all the irregularities, in the construction of
"any language, have arisen from the ellipsis of
"some words, which were originally inserted in
"the sentence, and [*which*] made it regular".

The word "*which*" is necessary here, because
when there is a change in the verbs, the nominative should be repeated; and, in Lindley
Murray's sentence, there is a change from a
passive to an active verb. He says;—"*words, which
"were originally inserted,* [there the verb is
"passive] *and* [*which*] *made it regular*"; [there
the verb is active]. Without the repetition of
the nominative "*which*", the sentence would

really read thus :—" words *which were* originally
" inserted, and [*which were*] made it regular"!

Lindley Murray himself says, on page 302 ;—
" When, in the progress of a sentence, we pass
" from the affirmative to the negative form, or from
" the negative to the affirmative, the subject or
" nominative is mostly, if not invariably, resumed.
" ...There appears to be, in general, equal reason
" for repeating the nominative, and resuming the
" subject, when the course of the sentence is
" diverted by a change in the mood or tense."

It is remarkable that Lindley Murray's error,
of *omitting* the pronoun "*which*", is in a sentence
concerning irregularities of language arising
from *ellipses*.

Many writers consider the repetition of a word
in a sentence, to be an inelegance. But though
variety gives vivacity to our expressions, it is not
always a beauty ; for, sometimes it obscures the
meaning ; and, at other times, it is positively
ungrammatical.

With regard to the repetition of relative pronouns, it is a rule that,

" Whatever relative is used, in one series of clauses,
" relating to the same antecedent, the same rela-
" tive ought generally to be used in them all."

Thus wrote Lindley Murray, on page 233, and illustrated his remarks by the following example : —" .It is remarkable, that Holland, against *which* "the war was undertaken, and *that*, in the "very beginning, was reduced to the brink of "destruction, lost nothing." He adds ;—" The "clause ought to have been, ' and *which* in the "'very beginning'."

Notwithstanding his having thus laid down the law; (which, by the way, he has done in ungrammatical language; for, the words, "*the* "*same relative*", are redundant:) we find him writing, on page 517 ;—

> "A sentiment *which* is expressed in accurate lan-
> "guage, and in a period, clearly, neatly, and well
> "arranged, always makes a stronger impression
> "on the mind, than one *that* is expressed in-
> "accurately".

On page 51, also, we find him writing thus :—

> "Those are called 'labials ', *which* are formed *by* the
> "lips; those 'dentals ', *that* are formed *with* the
> "teeth ".

He changes not only the pronoun, but also the preposition in the latter part of this sentence. He should have said ;—" Those are called

" 'labials', *which* are formed *by* the lips ; those
" ' dentals', *which* are formed *by* the teeth ".

Again, on page 35, he says ;—

> " The vocal semi-vowels may be subdivided into pure
> " and impure. The pure are *those which* are
> " formed entirely by the voice : the impure, *such*
> " *as* have a mixture of breath with the voice."

In this passage, the latter part of the sentence
should have the same pronoun as the former part.
Lindley Murray should have said ;—" The pure
" are *those which* are formed entirely by the
" voice ; the impure, *those which* have a mixture
" of breath with the voice."

In reading the following sentence, on page 315
of Lindley Murray's ' *Grammar* ', we are in doubt
at first, as to what the relative pronoun "*which*"
refers to :—

> " The propriety or impropriety of many phrases, in
> " the preceding as well as in some other forms,
> " may be discovered, by supplying the words
> " that are not expressed; *which* will be evident
> " from the following instances of erroneous con-
> " struction."

Lindley Murray's sentence is, itself, an " in-
" stance of erroneous construction". He should
have said ;—" *this* will be evident " ; for, " *which* ",
being both singular and plural, may refer either

to the circumstance, or to the words, spoken of;
whereas, "*this*", being singular only, must refer
to the circumstance.

One more example.   On page 425, Lindley
Murray says;—

> "Authors sometimes plead the difficulty of their
> "subject, as an excuse for their want of per-
> "spicuity. But the excuse can rarely, if ever,
> "be admitted.   For [,] whatever a man conceives
> "clearly, he may, if he will be at the trouble, put
> "it into distinct propositions, and express it
> "clearly to others: and upon no subject ought
> "any man to write, where he cannot think
> "clearly."

Lindley Murray evidently forgot, that, as
personal pronouns are used to supply the place
of nouns, there is not, except in emphatic sentences, any necessity for using, in the same part
of a sentence, both the noun, and the pronoun
which represents the noun: *e.g.*, Shenstone
says;—

> "My *banks they* are furnished with bees
> "Whose murmur invites one to sleep."—p. 284.

On page 234, Lindley Murray condemns the
error; yet, in the sentence of his which I have
quoted above, he falls into it; as a very few
words will show.   Omit the parenthetical clause

which is in his sentence, and you will find that
he says ;—" *Whatever* a man conceives clearly,
"he may put *it* into distinct propositions, and
"express *it* clearly to others ". The pronoun
" *it*", in each instance, should have been omitted.

The last clause of the sentence is equally
faulty; it reads thus :—" Upon no subject ought
"any man to write, *where* he cannot think
"clearly." " *Where*", being an adverb of place,
is unsuitably employed in this instance. Lindley
Murray should have said ;—" *Upon no subject*
"ought any man to write, *upon which* he cannot
"think clearly." We *write upon* a subject; and
we *think upon* a subject; but we cannot say that
we *think in* a subject. Yet that is what Lindley
Murray's language implies.

A strange error occurs on page 486. He there
says ;—

> " We shall enumerate the principal figures, and give
> " *them* some explanation. "

Of course he means ;—" and give some expla-
" nation *of them*."

These are, certainly, remarkable errors for an
author to commit when actually writing on the
improprieties of the English language.

CRITICISM IV.

LINDLEY MURRAY.

Dr. Blair says, and Lindley Murray quotes the words;—"All that regards the study of compo-"sition, merits the higher attention upon this "account, that it is intimately connected with "the improvement of our intellectual powers. "For I must be allowed to say, that when we "are employed, after a proper manner, in the "study of composition, we are cultivating the "understanding itself. The study of arranging "and expressing our thoughts with propriety, "teaches to think, as well as to speak accu-"rately."

It is evident, however, that all Lindley Murray's "study of arranging and expressing *his* thoughts "with propriety", did not teach *him* to speak accurately; at least, not accurately according to his own rules. Judging him by his own standard, he errs in the use of even the articles.

On page 320, he tells us that it is incorrect to

say;—"A house and orchard"; because as there is, in the expression, but one article, it is understood as referring to both nouns; and though we may say;—"*A* house", we may not say;—"*A* orchard". The expression, then, should be ;— "A house and *an* orchard". This being Lindley Murray's rule, let us see how his language conforms to it.

> Page 52.—"Words duly combined produce a sentence;
> "and sentences properly combined produce an
> "oration or discourse."

i.e., "*an* oration or [*an*] discourse"!

> Page 517.—"A sentiment which is expressed in ac-
> "curate language, and in a period, clearly, neatly,
> "and well arranged, always makes a stronger im-
> "pression on the mind, than one that is expressed
> "inaccurately, or in a feeble or embarrassed
> "manner."

i.e., "in *a* feeble or [*a*] embarrassed manner"!

> Vol. II., page 7.—"The compiler would have deemed
> "himself culpable, had he exhibited such sentences .
> "as contained ideas inapplicable to young minds,
> "or which were of a trivial or injurious nature."

i.e., "of *a* trivial or [*a*] injurious nature"!

It is the notion of *plurality*, contained in these passages, which necessitates the repetition of the article.

The repetition of the article is necessary in such a sentence as this also; I quote from page 408 :—

> "It is difficult, in some cases, to distinguish between "an interrogative and exclamatory sentence".

Say, rather ;—" between an interrogative and "*an* exclamatory sentence"; otherwise, the words will read as if they formed a part of an unfinished observation respecting an interrogative and exclamatory sentence, and a sentence of some other kind. But it would have been better still, to say ;—" between an interroga*tory* and an exclama*tory* sentence". Where practicable, the adjectives thus brought into contrast should be alike in form. There is a third error in this simple sentence: Lindley Murray says; " It is difficult, in some cases, to "*distinguish between*". He should have said ;— "*discriminate between*". We *distinguish* one thing *from another;* but we *discriminate between* two or more things. On page 498, he speaks of

> "explaining the *distinction,* between the powers of "sense and imagination".

We *make* a *distinction ;* but it is a *difference,* which we *explain.*

We have thus found that Lindley Murray repeatedly errs in the use of verbs, adverbs, adjectives, pronouns, and articles. Let us now see whether he is not equally faulty in his use of nouns, conjunctions, and prepositions.

First, then, with respect to nouns. He says, on page 145 ;—

> " *Will*, in the first person singular and plural, inti-
> " mates resolution and promising; in the second
> " and third person only foretells ".

He should have said, either ;—"in the second "and third *persons* ";—or, "in the second and "*the* third person". This was necessary in order to show that he was speaking of *two persons ;* the one, second; the other, third; and not of *one person*, both second and third; supposing that to be possible.

"The reader's knowledge", as Dr. Campbell (quoted by Lindley Murray, on page 258) observes, "may prevent his mistaking the language; but, "if such modes of expression be admitted where "the sense is clear, they may inadvertently be "imitated in cases where the meaning would be "obscure, if not entirely misunderstood." Besides, in the very next paragraph, Lindley Murray uses the correct noun: he says ;—"*Shall*, on the

"contrary, in the first person, simply foretells;
"in the second and third *persons*, promises,
"commands, or threatens."

An error, the exact reverse of that just referred to,
occurs on page 412. Lindley Murray there says;—

> "This character is chiefly used in the Old, and in the
> "New Testament*s*."

This is a very common error. Clergymen are
frequently heard saying;—"Let us sing the
"hundredth psalm, omitting the second and the
"third *verses*." Other clergymen, equally faulty
in grammar, say;—"Let us sing the hundredth
"psalm, omitting the second and third *verse*."
Both forms are wrong. When the noun is in the
plural, the article must *not be repeated* before the
second adjective: we should say;—"the second
"and third *verses*." But when the noun is in
the *singular*, the article *must be repeated* before
the second adjective: we should say;—"the
"second, and *the* third, *verse*." Lindley Murray
should have said;—"This character is chiefly used
"in the Old, and in the New, Testament."

We will now consider his errors in the use of
conjunctions. On page 465, we find him saying,
concerning connective particles;—

"They should not be *either* too frequently repeated,
"awkwardly exposed to view, or made up of
"polysyllables, when shorter words would as well
"convey the meaning."

Now, " *either*" means one of *two;* but Lindley
Murray has, in the sentence just quoted, used
it in speaking of one of *three*, and therefore has
misused it.   His sentence ought to have been ;—
"They should not be very frequently repeated,
"nor should they be awkwardly exposed to view,
"or be made up of polysyllables when shorter
"words would as well convey the meaning."

" *Whether*", also, refers to *two* only, and is, in
strictness, " *which of two*"; yet Lindley Murray
uses it in speaking of *four*, and says, on page
479 ;—

"It is requisite, that we fix in our mind a just idea of
"the general tone of sound which suits our
"subject; that is,......*whether* round and smooth,
"*or* stately and solemn, *or* brisk and quick, *or*
"interrupted and abrupt."

Some authors defend this use of the word; but
they do so, more on the ground of expediency,
than on that of grammatical accuracy.   I
should write Lindley Murray's sentence thus ;—
"It is requisite that we fix in our minds a just

D

"idea of the general tone of sound which suits
"our subject; that is, *whether* round and smooth,
"*or* interrupted and abrupt; *whether* brisk and
"quick, *or* stately and solemn."
On page 384, I read :—

> "We have before shown that the cæsura improves the
> "melody of verse; and we shall now speak of its
> "other [and] more important office, that of being
> "the chief source of harmony in numbers."

In this sentence, the necessity for the conjunction "*and*", after the word "*other*", will be
apparent to the most superficial reader.
On page 390, I read :—

> "Few precise rules can be given, which will hold,
> "without exception, in all cases; but much must
> "be left to the judgment and taste of the writer."

Lindley Murray should have said, either ;—"*A*
"*few* precise rules can be given, *but* much must
"be left to the judgment", etc.; or else ;—"*Few*
"precise rules can be given; much must be
"left", etc. The former expression has the article
"*a*" inserted before "*few*"; the latter expression
has the conjunction "*but*" struck out. "*A few*",
having an affirmative meaning, may be followed
by "*but*". Whereas, "*few*", having a negative

meaning, does not admit the conjunction "*but*" after it, in the sentence quoted above.

With regard to the conjunction "*that*"; Lindley Murray says, on page 323;—"There is a "very common ellipsis of the conjunction "*that*": as 'He told me [that] he would proceed "'immediately.' This ellipsis is tolerable in "conversation, and in epistolary writing, but it "should be sparingly indulged in [in] every other "species of composition." Lindley Murray's practice, however, is sometimes as follows; page 4:—

> "In its present form, the work is designed for the
> " use of persons, who may think [that] it merits
> " a place in their libraries."

Again, page 484:—

> "This cannot be called a resemblance between the
> " sense and the sound, seeing [that] long or short
> " syllables have", etc.

The copulative conjunction "*and*" is sometimes erroneously used instead of the disjunctive conjunction "*or*". For instance, on page 172, Lindley Murray says;—

> "It is obvious that *a language* like the Greek *and*
> " Latin", etc.

He should have said;—"a language like the "Greek *or the* Latin".

On page 30, also, the same error is found. Lindley Murray there says;—

> "A perfect alphabet of the English language, *and,*
> "indeed, of *every other language,* would contain
> "a numbers of letters, precisely equal to the
> "number of single articulate sounds belonging
> "to *the language.*"

He should have said;—"A perfect alphabet *of* "*the English language, or,* [not "*and*"] *indeed, of* "*any other language,* would contain", etc.

In the following sentence, taken from page 364, the conjunction "*as*", signifying "*that*", is apt to be mistaken for the adverb "*as*", signifying "*in the same manner*":—

> "Such pauses have the same effect *as* [better "*that*"]
> "a strong emphasis [has]; and are subject to the
> "same rules; especially to the caution just now
> "given of not ["*against*" would have been
> "better] repeating them too frequently."

Is a *rule* a *caution?* Lindley Murray says;— "subject to the same *rules; especially to the* "*caution* just now given".

Surely it is well to *caution* the public against being misled by such English as this.

Let us now look at some of Lindley Murray's sentences in which the conjunction "*both*" is used; and we shall find that he is at fault in those also :—

> Page 122.—"The perfect tense, and the imperfect
> "tense, *both denote* a thing that is past".

As he did not intend the conjunction to apply to the verb "*denote*", but to the perfect and imperfect tenses, he should have placed it before them, and have said;—"*Both the perfect tense and* "*the imperfect tense*, denote a thing that is past".

> Page 306.—"That *both the circumstances* of contingency
> "and futurity are necessary will be evident", etc.

This language implies that the writer was speaking, not of the circumstance of contingency and the circumstance of futurity, but, of *two circumstances of contingency*, etc. He should have said;—"That both the circumstance of "contingency and *that of* futurity are necessary, "will be evident", etc.

> Page 382.—"We shall consider each of these three
> "objects in versification, *both with respect* to the
> "feet and the pauses."

We naturally wonder at the "*pause*" at the

end of this sentence; for, the construction of it
leads us to believe that it is incomplete; and
that the writer intended to continue it thus:—
" *both with respect to* the feet and the pauses, *and*
" *with respect to* "—something else.   He should
have said;—" We shall consider each of these
" three objects in versification, with respect *both*
" *to the feet,* and *to* the pauses."

The same error occurs twice on page 125.
Lindley Murray there says;—

> " The present, past, and future tenses, may be used
> " either definitely or indefinitely, *both with re-*
> " *spect* to time and action."

Say, rather;—" with respect *both to time* and
" *to* action."

When the conjunction " *both* " is followed by a
preposition, that preposition must be repeated
after the conjunction " *and*", in the succeeding
part of the sentence; as,—" This, in philosophical
" writing, has a disagreeable effect, *both upon* the
" memory, *and upon* the understanding of the
" reader."—'*Lindley Murray's Grammar*', p. 193.

Lindley Murray's practice, however, is not
uniform.   He says, on page 153 ;—

> " In other languages, a principle of this nature has

"been admitted, *both in the* conjugation of verbs,
" *and* [in] *the* declension of nouns."

In the following sentence, the conjunction
"*both*" is redundant.

Page 329.—"Performing at the same time the offices
both of the nominative and objective cases."

If the conjunction "*both*" be retained, then the
sentence should be written thus:—"Performing
"at the same time the offices *both of the* nomi-
"native *and of the* objective *case*."

The teaching of the foregoing criticisms respecting the conjunction "*both*", may be sum-
med up thus:—

In a compound sentence formed with the conjunctions "*both*" and "*and*", if an article, or a
preposition, or both, follow the former, then that
article, or that preposition, or both, must be
repeated after the latter.

CRITICISM V.

LINDLEY MURRAY.

A BRIEF review of Lindley Murray's errors in the use of prepositions will conclude this part of our subject. We shall afterwards consider his errors in the structure of sentences.

With regard to prepositions, then, we find Lindley Murray writing as follows :—

> Page 61.—"A substantive may, in general, be dis-
> "tinguished by its taking an article before it, or by
> "its making sense *of* itself".

Say ;—"making sense *by* itself".

> Page 77.—"This gives our language a superior ad-
> " vantage *to* most others ".

Say ; — "an advantage *over* most others".
"*Superior advantage*" is tautology.

> Page 113.—"The *participle* is a certain form of the
> "verb, and derives its name from its *participating*,
> "not only *of* the properties of a verb, but also *of*
> "those of an adjective ".

Say ;—"*participating in*"; or, "*partaking of*".

Page 125.—" *In* respect of time ".

Say ;—" *With* respect *to* time "; as, indeed, Lindley Murray does say in the next paragraph.

Page 194.—" The Greeks were the greatest reasoners
" that ever appeared in the world; and their lan-
" guage, accordingly, abounds more than any
" other *in* connectives."

Say, either ;—"the language abounds *with* con-
"nectives"; or,—"connectives abound *in* the
"language."

Page 221.—" Independently *on* the rest of the
" sentence".

Say ;—" Independently *of* the rest of the
" sentence". We say ;—" pendent *from*", " de-
"pendent *on* ", "independent *of*".

Page 365.—"To render pauses pleasing and expressive,
" they must not only be made in the right place,
" but also [be] accompanied *with* a proper tone of
" voice".

Say ;—" accompanied *by* a proper tone of ·
" voice."

Page 441.—" A person thoroughly conversant *in* the
" propriety of the language ".

Say ;—" conversant *with* the propriety of the
" language".

Page 487.—"This being the case, we may see the "necessity *of* some attention ".

Say ;—"the necessity *for* some attention ".

It were easy to multiply instances of Lindley Murray's errors in the use of the different parts of speech. I have thought it sufficient to give *examples* of his errors. His numerous inconsistences are truly astonishing. On page 325, he says ;—" The examples that follow are produced "to show the impropriety of ellipsis in some par-"ticular cases : ' In the temper of mind he was "'then '; *i.e.*, ' *in which* he then was '. Again, "' The little satisfaction and consistency, to be "'found in most of the systems of divinity I "' have met with, made me betake myself to the "' sole reading of the Scriptures ': it ought to "be, ' *which are* to be found ', and ' *which* I have "'met with '." Yet, though Lindley Murray could thus teach others; he could say, on page 360 ;—

"Learning to read, in the best manner it is now "taught ".

He should have said ;—"in the best manner "*in which* it is now taught ".

Here, too, is a strange sentence for a grammarian to have written :—

> Page 367.—" Tones are different both from emphasis
> "[*emphases*] and [*from*] pauses; consisting of
> "[*and consist of*] the modulation of the voice,
> "[*or of*] the notes or variations of sound which
> "we employ in the expression of [*in expressing*]
> "our sentiments."

But the following specimen of awkward construction is even more strange :—

> Page 452.—"In every composition there is always
> "some connecting principle among the parts.
> "Some one object must reign and be predominant.
> "But most of all, in a single sentence, is required
> "the strictest unity."

First, "In every composition there is *always*
"some connecting principle among the parts."
Why say "*always*"? Whatever is in a composition, forms a part of it; consequently, whatever
is there once, is there always. You may alter
the composition; but if you alter it, it is no
longer the same composition. The word "*always*",
in Lindley Murray's sentence, is therefore redundant, and should be struck out. It would be
better to say, likewise;—"there is some *connexion*
"among the parts"; than to say;—"there is
"some *connecting principle* among the parts."

The next sentence is ;—" Some one object must "reign and be predominant." What grandiloquent nonsense is this? If an object can be said to *"reign"*, of course it is *"predominant".* Why could not Lindley Murray be content to say ;—" Some object must predominate"?

The concluding sentence is as follows ;—" But "most of all, in a single sentence is required the "strictest unity". Why all this inversion? Why not say ;—" But the strictest unity is required in "a single sentence"; or, "But it is in a single sentence that the strictest unity is required"?

On page 459, Lindley Murray tells us that ;— "The first rule for promoting the strength of a "sentence, is *to prune it of all redundant words* *"and members" ;* yet, within a very few pages of this remark, we find in his own language the following specimen of verbosity :—

> Page 452.—"In this sentence, though the objects
> "contained in it have a sufficient connexion with
> "each other, yet, by this manner of representing
> "them, by shifting so often both the place and the
> "person, *we* and *they*, and *I* and *who*, they appear
> "in so disunited a view, that the sense of con-
> "nexion is much impaired".

In this sentence, he has employed fifty-five

words, in order to express what might thus be expressed more clearly in thirty-two :—

"Although the objects in this sentence are "sufficiently connected, the frequent changing of "the pronoun—*we, they, I, who*—makes them "appear so disunited that the sense of connection "is much impaired". His sentence contains three-and-twenty words too many!

On page 461, Lindley Murray very properly objects to such tautological expressions as, "*Forced* to get home, partly by stealth, and "partly by *force*"; and, "The *universal* love and "esteem of *all* men". But, only three pages further on, we find him saying ;—

"'I came, I saw, I conquered', expresses, with more "force, the *rapidity* and *quick succession* of con-"quest, than if connecting particles had been "used."

Again, on page 498, he says, of certain impressions ;—

"*As soon as* they are made, they are *instantly* lost."

Concerning the order of words in a sentence, Lindley Murray says, on page 449;—"When "different things have an obvious relation to

"each other, in respect to the order of nature or
"time, that order should be regarded, in assign-
"ing them their places in the sentence; unless
"the scope of the passages require it to be
"varied. The conclusion of the following lines
"is inaccurate, in this respect: 'But still there
"'will be such a mixture of delight, as is pro-
"'portioned to the degree in which any one of
"'these qualifications is most conspicuous and
"'prevailing'. The order in which the two last
"[the last two] words are placed, should have
"been reversed, and made to stand, *prevailing*
"and *conspicuous.*—They are *conspicuous,* because
"they *prevail*".

I turn over one leaf only, and find that Lindley
Murray has quite forgotten all that he had said
about the order of the words in a sentence. On
page 453, he writes as follows:—

> "The violation of this rule tends so much to perplex
> "and obscure, that", etc.

Adopting Lindley Murray's own form of criticism, I say;—"The order in which the last two
"words are placed, should have been reversed,
"and made to stand, *obscure* and *perplex.* The
"*perplexity* is occasioned by the *obscurity.*"

Concerning precision, Lindley Murray says, on page 438 ;—

"It signifies *retrenching superfluities, and* pruning the expression, so as to exhibit *neither more nor less, than* an exact copy of the person's idea who uses it."

If Lindley Murray had borne in mind his own definition of *"precision"*, he would have struck out of his sentence the words printed in italics; for, what is meant by *"retrenching superfluities"*, but *"pruning the expression"*? and what is conveyed in the words *"neither more nor less"*, that is not conveyed in the word *"exact"*? But worse than all, is the expression,—*"the person's idea who"*! After *that*, the reader will be prepared for the assertion that almost every kind of fault in composition may be found in Lindley Murray's own writings; and yet, I affirm, he is not more inaccurate in his language, than are ninety-nine men out of every hundred. He knew what was correct in the use of words, and effected much good in his day, but his practice was strangely at variance with his precepts.

SECOND PART.

CRITICISMS,

ORIGINALLY PUBLISHED IN AMERICA,

ON

THE HON. GEORGE P. MARSH'S STRICTURES.

BAD ENGLISH EXPOSED.

CRITICISM VI.

THE HON. GEORGE P. MARSH.

THE Hon. George P. Marsh is contributing to
'*The Nation*' a series of articles on the new
edition of '*Webster's Dictionary*'; and the editor
of that periodical says, in a brief notice intro-
ducing the first of the series;—"We believe that
" they will be found the most valuable and enter-
" taining criticism which that work has yet elicited,
" and we commend them especially for perusal
" and preservation to the scholars and the whole
" corps of instructors of the country."

Knowing that Mr. Marsh's criticisms are deserving of attentive perusal, and that his opinions
will be received with deference by the most eminent philologists in Europe as well as in America,
I write, in the interests of literature, to request

E

that you will allow me, through the medium of
' *The Round Table*', firstly, to call attention
to those valuable criticisms themselves, and,
secondly and chiefly, to offer a word of caution
to young students against allowing themselves
to be tempted to adopt certain inaccuracies and
inelegancies which are discernible in Mr. Marsh's
sentences.

No person can doubt that Mr. Marsh is thoroughly conversant with the structure of the
English language, and that his errors in composition are simply the result of carelessness. But,
as many persons are apt to be misled by the
errors of great writers; and, as teachers even may
be inclined to defend those errors, on the ground
that the usage of our great writers is the only
standard of correctness in the language, it is
necessary to point out, that it is their usage in
their most highly-finished compositions only,
which can safely be accepted as the standard;
and that we ought not to regard any work as
faultless because of its bearing the signature of a
great name, for " *even old Homer sometimes nods*."

The Hon. George P. Marsh, will not, I am
sure, take offence when no offence is intended;
and he is too true a scholar to object to criticisms

on his own writings if, by means of those criticisms, any information can be imparted to youthful literary aspirants who are zealously pursuing those studies in which he has so honourably distinguished himself. He will readily admit that essays " on the character, composition, and " sources of the English language " ought to be written with such care, that the purity and lucidity of the expressions employed shall inclose, as in crystal, the living thoughts of the author's mind ; and if, in Mr. Marsh's essays, I point out here an obscuration of the meaning by the use of an inapt word, there a phrase rendered ungrammatical by the employment of an improper ellipsis, elsewhere an inverted clause causing a partial confusion of the thought, etc., etc., he will not, like a certain writer of less eminence who could not afford to acknowledge an error, set up a defence which his better judgment condemns ; and, by palliating an inaccuracy because it is his own, inflict a lasting injury on a language spoken by nearly one hundred millions of the human race.

Mr. Marsh begins his first essay thus :—

" I propose to contribute to '*The Nation*', in the form "indicated by the above heading [' *Notes on the* " ' *New Edition of Webster's Dictionary* '], a series

E 2

"of miscellaneous observations on the character,
"composition, and sources of the English lan-
"guage."

There is, in this passage, an error of very common ocurrence.   We hear it in conversation,
we meet with it in books and in periodicals, and
it is a particular favourite with English clergymen ; one of whom recently began a sermon
by saying ;—"I propose to make a few observa-
"tions on the character of the prophet Elijah."
I can imagine the astonishment that would have
been depicted in the speaker's countenance if one
of his congregation had risen and said ;—"I object
"to that proposal."   The clergyman, recovering
from his surprise, would, very probably, have ex-
cxclaimed with indignation ;—"Sir, this is neither
"the time nor the place for discussion.   I will
"hear you in the vestry when this service is
"concluded.   I did not make any proposal what-
"ever.   I stated simply that it was my intention
"to make a few observations on the character of
"the prophet Elijah."   That, no doubt, was
what he intended to do ; but certainly it was not
what he did.   His words were the proclamation
of a proposal :—"*I propose*" ; he wished them to
be the announcement of an intention, and should,

therefore, have said;—"*I purpose*". Mr. Marsh,
in like manner, was not making a proposal to
his readers; he was informing them of a course
which he intended to pursue.

A second error in Mr. Marsh's sentence is his
use of the adverb "*above*", as an adjective. He
says;—"the *above* heading". This mode of
expression has the sanction of many of our
best writers; but it cannot be defended on
grammatical grounds. Though what we could
advantageously substitute for the similarily
constructed expressions, "*up*-train", and "*down*-
train", I do not know.

With regard to the word "*propose*":—

Dr. Crombie says;—"When usage is divided, as
"to any particular words or phrases, and when
"one of the expressions is susceptible of a differ-
"ent meaning, while the other admits only cne
"signification, the expression which is strictly
"univocal should be preferred. To *purpose*, for
"'to intend', is better than to *propose*, which
"signifies also 'to lay before', or 'submit to con-
"'sideration'; and '*proposal*,' for a thing offered
"or 'proposed', is better than '*proposition*",
"which denotes also 'a position', or 'the affirm-
"'ation of any principle or maxim.' Thus we

"say, 'he demonstrated Euclid's *proposition*',
"and 'he rejected the *proposal* of his friend.'"—
' *Treatise on Etymology and Syntax* ', p. 324.

Mr. Marsh continues his essay thus :—

> "I select this dictionary as a basis for my remarks,
> "because its wide circulation has made it acces-
> "sible to all, and because, as it stands in this
> "edition, its vocabulary is more copious, its
> "etymologies more sound and satisfactory, and
> "its definitions more accurate than those of any
> "other English dictionary known to me."

The structure of this sentence appears to me to
be very faulty. Mark what is said in it concerning
the dictionary:—"Its vocabulary is more copious,
"its etymologies more sound and satisfactory,
"and its definitions more accurate". The reader
will perceive that there is here but one verb—the
verb "*is*"; and, as that governs the whole of
the clause, we really are told that the *etymologies
is* more sound, and the *definitions is* more accurate! Grammatical correctness requires that the
clause should run thus:—"Its vocabulary *is* more
"copious, its etymologies *are* more sound and
"satisfactory, and its definitions more accurate".
But the errors in this sentence do not end here,
for, the passage is thus continued :—"than those
"of any other English dictionary known to me";

that is, " its definitions are more accurate *than*
" *those of any other English dictionary known to*
" *me*" *;* its "etymologies are more sound and
" satisfactory *than those of any other English*
" *dictionary known to me*" *;* and (here is the
error) "its vocabulary is more copious *than those*
" *of any other English dictionary known to me.*"
Are there, then, some dictionaries having more
than one vocabulary? The fact is, that Mr.
Marsh has created difficulties for himself by
attempting, in one general expression, to draw
comparisons concerning certain nouns, two of
which are in the plural, while the other, unfortunately, is in the singular. The way to sur-
mount the difficulty is to put all the nouns in
the plural. This may be done by saying;—" In
" this edition *the words* of the vocabulary are
" more numerous, the etymologies more sound
" and satisfactory, and the definitions more accu-
" rate than those of any other English dictionary
" known to me." The expression " *as it stands* "
is redundant, and should, therefore, be struck out.
The next sentence in the essay is :—

"In all these respects the work is a great improve-
   "ment upon previous issues of that long familiar
   "to the literary world under the same name."

Here is a fault not of grammar, but of composition ; one against which we should be most carefully on our guard, because it confuses the reader's mind respecting the thought intended to be expressed. Mr. Marsh has connected, by position, words which are disconnected in meaning :—" *the literary world under the same name.*" The sentence should have been written thus :—
" In all these respects the work is a great im-
" provement upon previous issues of that which,
" under the same name, has long been familiar
" to the literary world."

In the next sentence but one, Mr. Marsh speaks of

" *a* historian ".

It is generally admitted that, when, in a word beginning with "*h*", the accent falls on the second syllable, the aspiration of the "*h*" is so much suppressed, that the word takes " *an*", instead of "*a*", before it.   Thus, we say ;—

a history, ... but *an* historian ;
a hero, ... but *an* heroic action ;
a heretic, ... but *an* heretical opinion ;
a habit, ... but *an* habitual drunkard ;
a harmony, ... but *an* harmonious sound ;
a herald,.......................... but *an* heraldic device ;

a heptagon, ... but *an* heptagonal figure ;
a hexagon,........................ but *an* hexagonal figure ;
a hydra, ... but *an* hydraulic press ;
a hypocrite, ... but *an* hypocrisy ;
a hyperbolical expression, ... but *an* hyperbole ;
a hypothetical position, ... but *an* hypothesis.

We say, also, *an* harangue, *an* hiatus, an hilarity, *an* horizon, *an* hyena, *an* hysterical person. The change of accent, from the first syllable to the second, neutralizes the aspiration of the "*h*". But before the words "*humane*", "*humidity*", and "*humility*" we do not use "*an*" but "*a*", because, although the accent is on the second syllable, and, consequently, the "h" is not sounded, we still have the sound of "*u long*", and therefore say;—"*a* humane man," "*a* "humidity," "*a* humility"; just as we say;—"*a* "united family", "*a* unanimous decision", etc. So, also, before the words "*humour*", and "*humourist*", we use "*a*"; not because those words begin with "*h*", for the "*h*" is mute; but because the "*u*", which immediately follows the "*h*", has the sound of the consonant "*y*".

CRITICISM VII.

THE HON. GEORGE P. MARSH.

In the line next to that in which **Mr. Marsh** speaks of *" a historian"*, I read :—

> "When, therefore, instead of exhibiting the oral or
> "written forms of a language, which have been
> "sanctioned by the ablest speakers and authors
> "in that language, he assumes to impose new or
> "unusual forms upon the tongue or the pen of
> "those whose breath it is, he is usurping func-
> "tions which belong to a higher jurisdiction, and
> "the greater the merits of his work may be
> "otherwise, the greater is the sin of his trans-
> "gression."

The conjunction *" or "* is not always used to contrast things which differ essentially; it is sometimes used where the difference is merely nominal; and good writers generally indicate, by one of the following methods, whether the difference is essential or nominal :—If, for the purpose of being more explicit in speaking of something, it is needful to mention it under two names; we then connect the names by *" or "* simply; we do not repeat the preposition or the article before the second name; we say;—"He "went to Van Diemen's Land or Tasmania"; and those who know the language, know that we are speaking of only one place, and that Tasmania is another name for Van Diemen's Land. But if we wish to speak of two places, we repeat the preposition, and say;—"He came from New "York or *from* Baltimore"; or we repeat the article, and say;—"The tongue or *the* pen"; or we prefix the word "*either*" to the former of the two, and say;—"*Either* new or unusual forms". In Mr. Marsh's sentence, which I have quoted at the beginning of this paragraph, he speaks of "the oral or written forms of a language"; but, as they are distinct and different, he ought to have said;—"the oral or *the* written forms of a "language". The repetition of the article is just as necessary in this place, as it is in that other part of the sentence, where Mr. Marsh says;— "the tongue or *the* pen". But there is an error of the same sort between these two quotations. Mr. Marsh says;—"When .. he assumes to impose "new or unusual forms upon the tongue or the "pen": he should have said;—"*either* new or "unusual forms"; for, an unusual form is not necessarily a new form. In confirmation of this opinion on the conjunction "or", see Dr. Campbell's '*Philosophy of Rhetoric*', Vol. ii, page 49. A third error in the sentence consists of an improper change in the mood of the verb. Mr. Marsh says;—"The greater the merits of his work *may* "*be* otherwise, the greater *is* the sin of his trans- "gression."   This should have been;—"The "greater the merits of his work *are* otherwise, "the greater is the sin of his transgression"; or, better still;—"The greater the merits which "his work *has* otherwise, the greater is the sin of "his transgression."

Mr. Marsh's '*Notes*' are thus continued :—

"In justice it should be added that where the Web-
"sterian orthography differs from that generally
"regarded as normal in England, the latter is
"given in brackets and small italics, in the pre-
"sent edition. This is an improvement, certainly,
"but it would have been much better and fairer
"to put the spelling adopted by the highest
"living and recent authorities at least upon an
"equal footing with that which the editors pro-
"pose to substitute for it, by assigning to it as
"conspicuous a place and letter as to the new
"orthography."

In this passage Mr. Marsh did not, I believe,

mean to speak of a certain orthography " re-
" garded as *normal in England* ", but of a certain
orthography *regarded in England* as normal. In
the latter part of the sentence Mr. Marsh falls
into a similar error, and tells us something which
is directly opposed to that which he wished to
express. He says ;—" It would have been much
" better and fairer to put the spelling adopted
" by the highest living and recent authorities at
" least upon an equal footing with that *which the*
" *editors propose to substitute for it, by assigning*
" *to it as conspicuous a place and letter as to the*
" *new orthography.*" We are told that the editors
of ' *Webster's Dictionary*' propose to substitute one
mode of spelling for an other, by giving to each an
equally conspicuous place and letter ! I venture
to suggest that Mr. Marsh's meaning would have
been more clearly expressed by the following
briefer form of words : — " This is an im-
" provement, certainly ; but it would have been
" much better and fairer to put both upon an ·
" equal footing, by assigning to the spelling
" adopted by the highest living and recent au-
" thorities, a place and letter as conspicuous as
" those which are assigned to the new orthography."
Nothing is unimportant in literary composi-

tion. As, in chess, the result of a game is frequently determined by the position of a pawn, so, in a sentence, a writer's meaning is frequently determined by the position of a comma. In Mr. Marsh's next sentence there should be a comma after the word "language"; and then we should not read of—

> "A word-book of *a living language not extending*
> "*beyond a single volume.*"

Passing over the next sentence, I read as follows :—

> "That which has been accomplished for some lan-
> "guages, and which is in process of accomplish-
> "ment for several others—namely, a complete
> "historical and expository lexicon of the speech
> "—so far from having been effected for the
> "English language by Webster and his improvers,
> "was not even attempted by them, nor, though
> "Johnson and Richardson, not to mention some
> "older and less famous laborers in the same
> "field, had large and liberal ideas upon the
> "possibilities of lexicography, has it ever been
> "seriously undertaken until it was commenced,
> "within the last ten years, by the London Philo-
> "logical Society."

In the first place, can we correctly speak of a lexicon as being "in process of accomplishment"?

Ought we not rather to speak of the *writing* of such a work as being in process of accomplishment? To accomplish is to complete, to fill up; and as a lexicon cannot be said to exist until it is completed, it appears to me that we can no more speak of a lexicon as being in process of accomplishment, than we can speak of anything that is completed, as being in process of completion. Towards the end of the sentence, Mr. Marsh says;—"nor *has* it ever been seriously under-"taken until it *was* commenced, within the last "ten years, by the London Philological Society." Why this change in the tense of the verbs? It surely cannot be justified. Mr. Marsh should have said;—"nor *had* it ever been seriously under-"taken until it was commenced, within the last "ten years, by the London Philological Society."

One of the most frequently recurring errors in Mr. Marsh's '*Notes*' is the improper omission of the article after the disjunctive conjunction "*or*". I have given one or two instances of this; here is another, which differs from those previously noticed, in that it has an adjective before the first noun; and therefore, as the article is not repeated after the "*or*", the construction of the sentence requires that we accept the adjective as

applying to the second noun as well as to the
first.   Mr. Marsh speaks of—

> "The revolutions of language which have thrown out
> "of use and into oblivion a vast multitude of
> "terms familiar, in different ages, to our litera-
> "ture and our daily speech, sometimes supplying
> "their places by new vocables, sometimes burying
> "them with the dead objects or ideas they stood
> "for."

If Mr. Marsh did not mean to speak of *dead
ideas* as well as of "dead objects", he should have
said —"sometimes burying them with the dead
"objects or *with the* ideas they stood for"; or,
"for which they stood."

CRITICISM VIII.

THE HON. GEORGE P. MARSH.

I REJOICE that my letters have called forth hostile criticism; because now, haply, we shall be able to blend amusement with instruction; and, by good-humouredly laughing at the faults which each writer commits, shall induce the public to join in our mirth, and to take an interest in a study which hitherto, perhaps, they have regarded as intolerably dull.

There is, in a recent number of ' *The Nation* ' a letter dated from Trinity College and signed " S." It purports to be a review of ' *Moon's English* '. I am always thankful for the criticisms of any one who shows, by his mastery over language, that his critical opinions are deserving of respect. But when a would-be critic of my language, is unable to see the faults in his own, I smile at the expression of his benevolent intentions; and, while thanking him very cordially for his proffered services, decline to place myself under his tuition.

F

The second sentence in the letter of my collegiate friend is as follows:—

> "Mr. Marsh is, of course, quite able to carry on a
> "contest with Mr. Moon triumphantly, if he
> "would be at the trouble to do it, and certainly
> "does not need to call for any assistance."

An *elegant* writer would have said;—"*trium-
"phantly to carry on a contest* with Mr. Moon",
and not, "to carry on a contest with *Mr. Moon
"triumphantly*". Besides, how can Mr. Marsh's
ability to carry on a contest be dependent on
his *will?* Mr. S. says that Mr. Marsh is "able
". . . *if* he would", etc. But that is not all;
for, Mr. S. adds, "and certainly does not need to
"call for any assistance." That is, Mr. Marsh
is able "*if he* would be at the trouble to do it,
"and [*if he*] certainly does not need to call for
"any assistance." Mr. S. ought to have said;—
"and *he* certainly does not need to call for
"any assistance." But, as the sentence stands,
we are told that Mr. Marsh's *ability* to carry on
a contest with Mr. Moon triumphantly, is
dependent on the possession of two things : the
will to be at the trouble, and the *certainty* of his
not needing to call for any assistance. Should
he fail in either of these matters, his triumph

would, in the judgment of Mr. S., be doubtful! Well, after all, Mr. S. may be right; for, certainly, if Mr. Marsh needed *his* assistance, the case would indeed be a hopeless one.

I will examine the composition of another sentence of Mr. S.'s, and then proceed to investigate some of his critical opinions. In the same paragraph as that from which I just now quoted, I read :—

> "Perhaps his [Mr. Moon's] carelessness is due to the
> "fact that he is writing for Americans, of whose
> "ability to speak or write the English correctly
> "he has, at times, been hardly able to conceal his
> "doubts."

I am constrained to protest, here, against the injustice of this remark. I have, on every occasion, stood up in defence of the Americans; and those who know me and have read ' *The Dean's* ' *English* ', can bear witness to the truth of this assertion. It is the Dean of Canterbury who has maligned the people whose first President's name I am proud to bear. This is by way of parenthesis. Now let us examine the structure of the sentence. " To speak or write " should be, " to speak or *to* " write "; the actions are different, therefore the preposition should be repeated after the disjunctive conjunction "*or*"; and then, "to speak or "write *the English*" should, unquestionably, be "to speak or to write *English*". "*English*" means the language; "*the English*" means the people. We can no more speak "*the English*", than we can speak "*the Americans*".

Mr. S. objects to the word *co*temporaries". I really do not know how that word came to be printed in my letter in '*The Round Table*'. I am certain that in the manuscript which I sent to America I did not say;—

"the pages of *one of your cotemporaries*";

I said;—"the pages of '*The Nation*'". As for the word "*co*temporaries", which Mr. S. hopes may not take root, and which, he says, Dr. Bentley called "a down-right barbarism", Dr. Ogilvie, one of our best lexicographers, says, in his dictionary;—

"Contemporary, see *Co*temporary, the prefer- "able word."

Mr. S. appears to think that

"The general use in words compounded with the "inseparable preposition *con* is to retain the *n* "before a consonant and to expunge it before a "vowel or an *h* mute."

Indeed? How happens it, then, that we say;—
co-bishop, *co*-herald, *co*-guardian, *co*-partner,
co-worker, *co*-surety, *co*-defendent, *co*-lessee, *co*-
trustee, *co*-tenant, *co*-regent, etc., etc.? Why do
we say *co*habit, and not *con*habit? Why do we
say *co*vet, and not *con*vet? Why do we say *co*-
venant, and not *con*venant? The first syllable
of each of these words is from the Latin *con*,
and the second syllable begins with a consonant.
If Mr. S. should ever be on a jury, he would,
doubtless, make his *co*-jurors *conjurors;* and
were he speaking of the *co*-founders of the great
American Republic, he would call them *con-
founders!*

Mr. S. objects also to my use of the word

"fault",

as applied to grammar and to composition,
and would substitute the word *"error";* assigning as his reason, that *"error* respects the ·
" act, fault respects the *agent."* I suppose, then,
that geologists ought not to call a dislocation of
part of the earth's crust *"a fault"*, but *" an
"error"!* Will Mr. S. have the goodness to
suggest the alteration to his geological friends?

He condemns my use of the preposition "*of*" in the phrase,

"not a fault of grammar, but of composition",

and would substitute *in* for *of*. But "a fault *of* "composition" is one thing; and "a fault *in* "composition" may be quite an other thing. *Of* relates to *source*, whereas *in* relates to *place*. A fault *of* composition must, of course, be a fault *in* composition; but a fault *in* composition is not, necessarily, a fault *of composition*. It may be a fault *of grammar*. Mr. S. seems to know of only one meaning to the word "*of*", namely, that of possession; for he asks;—"Whose "error "*of* composition was it? Was it the compo-"sition's error?" This is worse than childish. Does Mr. S. really believe that "*the fear of the* "*Lord*" means that there is a feeling of fear in the mind of the Almighty? Is *this* what is taught at Trinity College? O fie!

With similar short-sightedness Mr. S. stumbles over the very obvious meaning of the same preposition, as it is used in the expression,

"the signature *of* a great name."

Of has at least a dozen significations; and, in

the foregoing expression, I have used it in the
sense of *consisting of.*

Mr. S. would substitute *"scholar"* for *"name"*.
I do not see any necessity for the change. My
expression is sanctioned by the example of the
author of ' *The Grammar of English Grammars* ',
who says, on page 36;—"It was not supposed
"that any reader would demand for every thing
" of this kind *the authority of some great name.*"

Mr. S. objects likewise to the expression,

"too *true* a *scholar*",

and says;—"Hobbs and Whately declare that
"only *assertions* can be *true* or false." In the
first place, Mr. S. has mistaken the meaning of
the word *"true"*, as used here. I do not speak
of Mr. Marsh's *veracity;* but, of his *faithfulness.*
Has Mr. S. never met with that meaning of the
word? Has he never read in the history of
Joseph;—"We are all one man's sons; we are
"*true men;* thy servants are no spies "? Has Mr.
S. never heard of the *"true God"?* I commend
to Mr. S., for his attentive perusal, an old-
fashioned book called " *The Bible* ".

Mr. S. has, evidently, no keenness of perception of the niceties of meaning conveyed in

terms which appear to be nearly synonymous. I had spoken of my wish

> "to offer a word of caution to young students *against*
> "*allowing themselves to be tempted* to adopt certain
> "inaccuracies",

and Mr. S. very innocently says;—"Does he "mean anything more than to offer a word of "caution to young students *against adopting* cer-"tain inaccuracies?" Certainly I do. I mean very much more. Does Mr. S. not know the meaning of even the *word* "temptation"? Or would he wish me to take the opposite view of the matter, and infer that, in his experience, to be tempted, and to yield to the temptation, are one and the same thing?

I am aware that

> "*purpose*" and "*propose*"

are derived from the same Latin word; but, like many other words which come from one common root, they differ in signification, and differ far more than do the kindred words, "*proposal*" and "*proposition*". Of these Mr. S. says;—"A *pro-* "*position*, when acceded to, is followed by an act "on the part of *those to whom it is submitted.* A "*proposal*, when accepted, is followed by an act

" on the part of *the proposer* ". I do not know whether Mr. S. rejoices in a state of single blessedness or not; but if he does, and if he should one day be " *tempted* ", by a pair of bright eyes, to make a *proposal* of marriage; I hope that he will experience that his *proposal* is followed by a very loving act on the part *of the fair one;* and that he will live to find that, not only an *assertion*, but also a *woman*, can be *true*.

CRITICISM IX.

THE HON. GEORGE P. MARSH.

THERE are many persons to whom the study of
language is distasteful ; and who, consequently,
have refused to acquaint themselves with the
properties of nouns, adjectives, adverbs, etc.;
but who, nevertheless, from a constant perusal
of our best authors, write and speak with comparative purity. Occasionally, however, they
are asked to decide respecting some disputed
point in grammar, and to give a reason for their
decision ; and they then, having no substantial
foundation of linguistic knowledge on which to
base an opinion, are obliged to confess their
ignorance of the laws of the language ; and so,
from the proud position of umpires, to which
their imagined mastery of those laws had raised
them in the estimation of their fellow-men, they
fall at once to the humiliating position of those
who are wilfully ignorant. There are other persons who have, for years, made language their

study; and who know the use of every "part of "speech", and can quote every rule of syntax; and yet, either from a want of keenness of perception, or of a proper sense of order in the arrangement of their thoughts, are unable to express their meaning with clearness and accuracy: and, from this cause, it comes to pass that the most obvious of all grammatical rules—that which refers to position—is the one which is most frequently violated.

It is possible to construct a sentence in which every word shall be wrong, and yet the meaning be manifest; it is also possible to construct a sentence in which every word shall be correct, and yet the meaning be obscure; and however much we may shrink from such vulgarisms as

"them's them",

we must admit that, since the object of all speech is the clear expression of our thoughts, he who, in the language he employs, is grammatically wrong but does not offend against perspicuity, is less culpable than he who, having received a certain amount of education, leaves the hearer, or the reader, in doubt as to the meaning intended to be conveyed. In the

phrase "*them's them*", each of the three words
is wrong. You cannot say,—"them *is*"; nor
can you say,—" *them* are"; neither can you
say,—"are *them*". You cannot say the first, because the verb "*is*" does not agree here with
that which governs it; you cannot say the
second, because "*them*" is accusative, and the
verb requires a nominative; and you cannot say
the last, because the verb "*to be*" should have
the same case after it as it has before it; therefore if the first "*them*" is incorrect, so is the
last; and thus we see that every word is incorrect.

Still, no person could be in doubt as to the
speaker's meaning; but when Mr. Marsh tells
us that there is

> "another difficulty in the way of all attempts to fix
> "the force of words belonging to the vocabulary
> "of our moral and intellectual nature by descrip-
> "tion",

we are obliged to pause for a moment, to consider
whether we rightly understand what is said;
and it is not until we are satisfied that Mr.
Marsh does not mean;—"belonging to the
"vocabulary of our moral and intellectual nature

"by description", that we perceive the last two words to be misplaced, and that he means, that there is "another difficulty in "the way of all attempts *to fix by description* "the force of words belonging to the vocabulary "of our moral and intellectual nature."

In the passage preceding the one which I have just quoted, Mr. Marsh uses a verb in the singular, when speaking of nouns in the plural; and, in a passage subsequent to it, he uses a verb in the plural, when speaking of a noun in the singular. The former of these passages is as follows :—

> "Language rises above even organization, for it is
> "animated not only by a vital but by a con-
> "trolling spiritual element, and its signification
> "*is* as varied as [*is*] the passions, the affections,
> "and the conceptions of the soul which inspires
> "it."

Of course it should be ;—" its significance *is* "as varied as *are* the passions, etc." The other passage is :—

> "These operations and affections are often but dimly
> "conscious even to ourselves, and the words by
> "which we indicate them *are* necessarily as inca-
> "pable of analysis as [*are*] the thing signified."

This should be;—"the words by which we indi-
"cate them *are* necessarily as incapable of analysis
"as *is* the thing signified." But in the beginning also of the sentence there is an error which
should not pass without comment. Mr. Marsh
says ;—These operations and affections are often
"but dimly conscious even to ourselves". This
is a very strange clause for so eminent a
philologist as Mr. Marsh to write. How can
"operations and affections" be "*conscious*"?
And if conscious, how can they be conscious
"*to*"? We may speak of *ourselves* as being *conscious of* certain operations and affections : or we
may speak of certain "*operations and affections*"
as being *perceptible* to us ; but we cannot speak of
their being *conscious* to us. Probably Mr. Marsh
meant to say, either ;—"These operations and
"affections are often but dimly perceptible even
"to ourselves"; or, "of these operations and
"affections we, ourselves, are often but dimly
"conscious."

Can either the relative pronoun "*who*", or its
possessive, "*whose*", correctly be employed concerning inanimate objects? I think not. Of
the relative pronouns, "*who*" and "*whose*" apply
either to persons, or to things personified;

"*which*" applies to irrational animals, to inanimate objects, and sometimes to infants; and "*that*" is used to prevent too frequent a repetition of "*who*" and of "*which*", and applies equally to persons, to animals, and to things. Such is our modern usage; and to it we ought to conform. I am aware that, in olden time, it was the custom to use "*which*" when speaking of persons; hence the phrase;—" Our Father *which* " art in heaven ". It was likewise the custom to say " whose ", when speaking of things; hence, in the opening lines of *Paradise Lost*, we read :—

> " Of man's first disobedience, and the fruit
> Of that forbidden tree *whose* mortal taste ".

But now, the best writers, when speaking of inanimate objects, use "*of which*" instead of "*whose*"; and I am surprised to find Mr. Marsh saying ;—

> "How can we define *that whose* being, whose action,
> " whose conditions, whose limitations we cannot
> "comprehend ? "

Would it not have been better to say ;—" How " can we define that, *of which* we cannot comprehend the being, the action, the conditions, the " limitations ? " ?

I know of no word in the English language

that is treated more as a drudge than is the
little word " *same* ".   It is laid under tribute for
all kinds of work, and has to do duty upon all
sorts of occasions.   It is found in penal enact-
ments; and, respecting the law, trespassers are
told what they will incur if they violate " *the*
" *same* ".   Young ladies, too, whose letters begin
with " *Dearest* ", and end with some message of
love, usually request their friends to accept " *the*
" *same* " themselves.   If a costermonger loses his
donkey, or if an old maid loses her fan, you are,
in each case, equally sure to read in the advertise-
ment that a reward will be paid for the recovery
of " *the same* ".   But, hard as it is to have to do
the work of other persons, it is still harder to have
to do work that is utterly useless; and the little
word " *same* " is frequently dragged in to do even
that.   Of what use is the word in the following
sentence of Mr. Marsh's ?—

" The higher the culture of a people, the larger will
    " be the proportion of indefinable words in its
    " [*? their*] language, and the signification of this
    " class of its words can be mastered only by the
    " *same* process by which the infant learns the
    " meaning of the vocabulary of the nursery, ob-
    " servation, namely, of actual living usage."

Strike out from this passage the word " *same* ", and what is lost, either in fulness of meaning or in euphony of language? Nothing. Nevertheless, if a writer wishes to emphasize the statement that it is by the *same* process, let him say ;—" by the " same process *as that* by which the infant ", etc. One more word respecting this sentence;—the last clause is dualistic ; and, as the one part is explanatory of the other, nothing could be easier than to arrange the words in their simple and proper order ; the pivot word being, the adverb " *namely* ". But, in Mr. Marsh's sentence, that word is misplaced ; and, as a natural consequence, his collocation of the words makes them grate on the ear. How much better it would have been to speak of mastering the difficulties " by the same process as that by which " the infant learns the meaning of the vocabulary " of the nursery, namely, observation of actual " living usage."

I close this letter by adding a few words on the expression

" *Dearest* ",

of which I have just spoken. A gentleman once

G

began a letter thus, to his bride :—" My *dearest* "Maria". The lady replied :—"My dear John, I "beg that you will mend either your morals "or your grammar. You call me your '*dearest* "'Maria'; am I to understand that you have "other Marias?"

It is said that, ever afterwards, John very properly addressed her as " Maria, my dearest".

CRITICISM X.

THE HON. GEORGE P. MARSH.

I FINISHED the first criticism in this series by commenting on Mr. Marsh's expression,— "*a* his-" "torian". Much more might have been said on the proper use of the article

"*a*" or "*an*", .

but I feared that, if I extended my remarks on that subject, I should weary the readers of '*The* '*Round Table*', and incur the charge of prolixity. However, as, in the last number which I have received of that journal, a correspondent at Washington asks for information concerning those important little words, I gladly resume my remarks on them; for, as I said, my purpose in writing these criticisms is not to expose Mr. Marsh's errors, but to base upon those errors such teaching as may be useful to students of the English language.

Lindley Murray and many other grammarians tell us that "*a*" becomes "*an*" before a vowel and before a silent "*h*"; but, what is really the

G 2

fact, is the converse of that. "*An*" becomes "*a*" before a consonant sound ; for, "*an*" is the original word, and was formerly used both before consonants and before vowels, and was not abbreviated to "*a*" until long after the Conquest. Dr. Webster says that in '*Saxon Chronicles*', page 82, we read ;—"And thæs geares wærun ofslegne IX "eorlas and *an* cyning"; *i.e.*;—And this year were slain nine earls and *one* king. But though the primary signification of "*a*" and of "*an*" is "*one*", Dr. Webster, in whose praise Mr. Marsh is writing, is certainly in error when he says, ('*Improved Grammar*', page 13);—"The definitive "'*an*' or '*a*' is merely '*one*', in its English or- "thography, and is precisely synonymous with "it". There is an obvious difference between the two words. We use "*one*" when we speak numerically, and wish to signify that there are not more than one; whereas we use either "*a*" or "*an*" when we wish to emphasize, not the *number*, but, the *description* of the thing spoken of. For example, were we to ask;—"Is chess a "game for *one boy* ? " the very natural and proper answer would be;—"No; it is to be played by "*two*." But were our question to be ;—"Is chess "a game for *a boy* ?"the answer would be ;—

"Yes; or for a girl." In this respect our language has a decided superiority over other languages; in them, one word performs the office both of what grammarians term an *article*, and of a *numeral*. In French, for instance, *Donnez moi un livre* means either;—Give me *one book; i.e.*, not two or more; or it means ;—Give me *a book*, not something else. In Latin, likewise ;—"*filius*" "*regis*" may mean ;—"*A* son of *a* king", "*A* son of "*the* king", "*The* son of *a* king", or "*The* son "of *the* king"; and if we wish to explain, in English, which of these four senses the expression is intended to convey, we have to employ several additional words. It is a curious fact, mentioned in a recent number of '*The Athe-*'*næum*', that we English alone of all nations, ancient or modern, have a *bonâ fide* article which is distinct from "*one*", though contracted from "*one*" and meaning "*one*". No nation but ourselves could use such expressions as ;—"Give "me half *a one*", "Not such *a one* as that", "Give me *a* ripe *one*". That "*a*" is not synonymous with "*one*", is evident from our not being able to use it interchangeably with "*one*". We may say ;—"This *one* thing I do"; but we cannot say ;—"This *a* thing I do",

But although "*a*" is not synonymous with "*one*", it always implies unity; and can therefore never be used but in speaking of *one*, or in speaking of *many* things *collectively; i.e.*, of *many* things considered as *one*. We say "*a one*", "*a thousand*", "*a quantity*", "*a number*", *a multi-* "*tude*". But though we say "*a multitude*", which means *many*, we never say "*a many*". Yet, by a strange caprice of idiom, we say "*a great many*", "*a few*", and "*many a*"; as :—

> "Full *many a* gem of purest ray serene
> The dark unfathomed caves of ocean bear;
> Full *many a* flower is born to blush unseen,
> And waste its sweetness on the desert air."
>
> GRAY.

This form is allowable in poetry; but in prose, it is generally preferable to say ;—"*many gems*", "*many flowers*".

While speaking of "*a few*", it is worthy of remark that the importance of the little word "*a*" is never more manifest than when it precedes the word "*few*"; for, the word "*a*" so qualifies it, that it signifies something quite different, when written without the "*a*", from what it does when written with it; *e.g.* :—

"*Few* persons really believe it;—it is incredible."

"*A few* persons really believe it;—it is *not* in-
" credible."

The same remark applies to "*little*" and "*a*
"*little*"; *e.g.*:—

" He thought *little* about it;—it was a matter
" of indifference to him."

" He thought *a little* about it;—it was *not* a
" matter of indifference to him."

When we use the words "*few*" and "*little*"
without "*a*" before them, we represent that of
which we speak, as being inconsiderable; but
by using "*a*" before them, we amplify—we
represent the thing spoken of as *not* being inconsiderable.

There is another important use of the word
"*a*" which we must notice. If we say;—" He
" would make a better statesman than lawyer",
we mean that he has qualities which render
him more fitted for the senate than for the
bar; but if we say;—" He would make a better
" statesman than *a* lawyer", we mean that he
would make a better statesman than a lawyer
would.

Again, when we speak of a man as holding
several offices at once, we put "*a*" before only

the first of those offices; as:—"a director, secre-
"tary, and treasurer." Were we to put "*a*"
before each of the names, we should no longer
be speaking of *one* man holding *three* offices, but
of *three* men, each holding *one* office. So, likewise, is it with words descriptive of qualities;
e.g.:—"A long and dusty road" is a road which is
both long and dusty; but, "A long and *a* dusty
"road" means two roads; of which one is long,
and the other dusty. However, when the things
spoken of are obviously two or more, there is not
the same necessity for repeating the article before
each one.

The article "*a*" has several meanings. Sometimes it means "*each*"; as:—"The high priest
"shall make an atonement for the children of
"Israel, for all their sins, once *a* year", *i.e.*,
once *each* year. Sometimes it means "*any*"; as:—
"If *a* man love me, he will keep my words";
i.e., if *any* man. Sometimes it means "*one in particular*; as:—"He sent *a* man before them, even
"Joseph." Sometimes it means "*every*"; as:—
"It is good that *a* man should both hope and
"quietly wait for the salvation of the Lord";
i.e., *every* man.

Sometimes "*a*" is used before the name of a

person; as:—" He is *a* Smith "; meaning he is of
the family of the Smiths. Here, in *written* language, the capital letter at the beginning of the
name shows it to be that of a person, and not of
a trade. But in *spoken* language the distinction
cannot be so easily made; therefore, in conversation, that form of expression should be avoided;
for if, in answer to my inquiry,—" Who is that? "
I am told;—" He is *a* Smith ", I am doubtful
whether my informant is speaking of the person's
family, or of his occupation; and if the name
should happen to be that of an animal; as, for
instance,—"Bull", or " Fox ";—it would be particularly offensive to say;—" He is *a* Bull", or "He
"is *a* Fox"; for—though, of course, the hearer
would not understand the person to be a quad-
ruped—the words might be understood to mean
that he is ferocious or is cunning. The proper
expression would be;—" He is a *Mr.* Smith ", or,
" a *Mr.* Fox."

But " *a* " is very properly used before the
name of a person whose extraordinary qualities
have made his name proverbial for that in which
he excelled. For example, we say;—" He is *a*
" Samson ", meaning, he possesses almost super-
human strength;—" He is *a* Nero", meaning, a

tyrant;—"He is *a* Howard", meaning, a philan-
thropist;—"He is *a* Washington", or "He is *a*
"Cincinnatus", meaning, a patriot.

There is a misuse of the article "*a*", which
is very common:—the employing it before the
word "*most*". The words are incongruous;
"*a*" means one of several which are supposed to
be equal in certain respects; whereas, "*most*" is
indicative of that which is above all.

"*An*" should always be used when the following word begins with the unaspirated "*h*", or
with any of the vowels, except

1st, "*u*" *when long, as if preceded by the letter*
"*y*". *e.g.*:—

we say;—a U, a Unitarian, a usurer, a usurious
rate of interest, a usurper, a use, a unicorn, a
utopian theory, a unit, a union, a uniform, a
university, a united family, a unanimous decision,
a unanimity, a utilitarian, a upas tree, etc.

2nd, "*eu*" *having the sound of "u" long; e.g.*:—
we say;—a eunuch, a eulogy, a euphemism, a
euphony, a European, etc.

3rd, "*ew*" *having the sound of "u" long; e.g.*:—
we say;—a ewe, a ewer, etc.

4th, "*o*" *when pronounced as if preceded by*
"*w*"; *e.g.*:—

we say;—a one-pound note, a oneness, such a one, a once-beloved friend, etc.

We use "*an*", likewise . before consonants which are pronounced as if they begin with a vowel; *e.g.:*—we say an F, an L, an M, an N, an R, an S, an X. Many grammarians say, also;—an H; and, in naming that letter, call it "*aitch*"; although it would, clearly, be more in accordance with its most frequent use, to call it "*h*aitch".

CRITICISM XI.

THE HON. GEORGE P. MARSH.

THE Hon. George P. Marsh is singularly unfortunate in having such a champion as Mr. S.,
of Trinity College, to do battle on his behalf.
When will men learn that the maintaining a dig-
nified silence respecting the faults of a friend, is a
truer kindness to him, than the entering the lists
in his defence, otherwise than fully armed for the
overthrow of his opponent? Mr. Marsh suffers
nothing from my criticisms. I freely concede
that the errors in his '*Notes*' are not those of
ignorance, but of inadvertence. The great
scholar has, doubtless, been more intent upon
pointing out the derivation of words, than upon
arranging them in their proper order in his
sentences. But he does suffer from the offi-
ciousness of his friends; because the world,
whether justly or unjustly I need not stop to
inquire, generally associates a man, for good
or for evil, with those who make common cause
with him.

Mr. S. thus writes to ' *The Nation* ' :—

> " Mr. Moon has written to ' *The Round Table* ', ' *to*
> " ' *base upon those errors such teaching* as may be
> " ' useful to students of the English language.'
> " I do not often find writers acknowledging that
> " their teaching is based on errors. When Mr.
> " Moon, therefore, avows that it is his ' purpose '
> " thus to base his teaching, I gladly call attention
> " to his honesty."

Would that I could return the compliment, and " call attention " to Mr. S.'s honesty; but, unfortunately, he has deprived me of the power of doing that, and I am reluctantly compelled to " call attention " to his *dis*honesty. He begins his letter by quoting *a part* of one of my sentences ; and, with an ingenuity which does him but little credit, he wrests out of the quotation, a meaning which the entire sentence would never convey. Mr. Marsh's advocate sacrifices his dignity as a scholar, and his truthfulness as a man, in a vain attempt to be witty.

Mr. S.'s next sentence is as follows :—

> " And after reading his article, I am ready to admit
> " that he accomplishes his purpose. His criti-
> " cism is upon the proper use of the *articles*
> " [? article] " *a* " and " *an* '."

Upon this passage I remark that it is not scholarly to begin a sentence with the copulative conjunction " *and* "; nor is it in good taste to use one word in two different senses in two consecutive lines, as Mr. S. does when he speaks of "reading his *article*......upon the proper use of "the *article*".

But there is an other error in the sentence preceding that which I have just noticed. Mr. S. says;—"I do not often find......When Mr. "Moon, therefore, avows", etc. The reader will observe that Mr. S., by putting the adverb "therefore" *after* my name, makes my avowal consequent upon his not finding, etc! He ought to have said;—"Therefore, when Mr. Moon avows"; not,—"When Mr. Moon, therefore, avows". Adverbs should be placed as near as possible to the words with which they are the most closely connected in meaning.

Mr. S.'s letter is continued thus:—

> "He has spread over two columns of ' *The Round*
> "' *Table*' that which, so far as his statements are
> "correct, might have been as clearly expressed
> "in one half the space."

As this is a comparative clause of *equality,*

Mr. S. ought to have said;—"*as* far as his state-"ments are correct". Again, Mr. S. ought not to have said;—"*one half* the space;—but, "*half* "the space." The word "*one*" is redundant, for there are but two halves in a whole; and, if we meant both, we should not use the word "*half*".

Mr. S. objects to my saying;—

> "I finished the first criticism in this series *by* com-"menting", etc.;

and he says of me;—"He blunders in the "use of the preposition '*by*'. '*Commenting*' "was not the agent or instrument *by* which he "finished his criticism. He should say; 'I "'finished the first criticism in this series *with* "'a comment'," etc. In nothing is the shallowness of Mr. S.'s knowledge of English more apparent than in his remarks concerning prepositions. He fails to see that the *improved* sentence not only does not convey my meaning, but that it is, in itself, really ambiguous. To finish "*a* "*criticism with a comment*" may mean to finish a criticism *containing a comment*. But to finish a criticism "*by commenting*" is to make the comment the finish or end of the criticism; and that was the meaning intended to be conveyed.

"*With*" is one of the most ambiguous prepositions in the language; *e.g.*:—"I killed a man
"*with* a sword." This may mean, either;—"A
"man *having* a sword was killed by me"; or,—
"I, *by means of* a sword, killed a man." Again,—
"He that is not *with* me is *against* me": Matt.
xii, 80. In this passage, "*with*" is opposed to
"*against*"; but in the following passage it is
identical with "*against*":—"In the days of Saul
"they made war *with* the Hagarites, who fell by
"their hand": 1 Chron. v, 10. *To make war
with* the Hagarites was *to fight against* them; but
when it is said, in Prov. xx, 18;—"*with good advice
"make war*", the meaning is certainly not that
we are *to fight against good advice!* Will Mr. S.
think me rude if I say, that his advice, with
respect to the use of prepositions, is something
against which it is wise to fight?

Concerning my sentence,

"*An* becomes *a* before a consonant sound",

Mr. S. says;—"It would be sufficient to say, '*An*
"'becomes *a* before a consonant.'" The fallacy
of this statement is easily shown. F, L, M, N,
R, S, and X, are consonants; and if "*an* becomes
"*a* before a consonant", as Mr. S. asserts, then

we ought to say ;—*a* F, *a* L, *a* M, *a* N, *a* R, *a* S,
and *a* X; a statement which needs only to be
mentioned in order to bring ridicule upon the
utterer. But *an* does become *a* before a consonant *sound*, even though the letter having that
sound is a vowel; *e.g.:*—we say, "*a* U", not "*an* U".
  With the expression

"a consonant sound",

Mr. S. finds fault, alleging that as "consonant"
means "harmonizing together", a "consonant
"sound" is an "harmonious sound"; and that
I ought to have said ;—"a consonantal sound".
This is another instance of Mr. S.'s short-
sightedness. The word "*consonant*", in the
expression "*a consonant sound*", is not an adjective, meaning "*harmonious*", but is a noun and the
name of certain letters of the alphabet; and "*a
consonant sound*" is the sound of a consonant.
It is just as correct an expression as is either
"*a vowel sound*" or "*a thunder clap*". I suppose
that they say at Trinity College, "a vowel*al*
"sound", and "a thunder*al* clap"! *Apropos* of
Mr. S.'s tautological expression

"*harmonizing together*";

H

I should much like to know how sounds can
harmonize otherwise than *together.*

My critic of Trinity College thus continues
his remarks :—

> "Mr. Moon writes, 'We use *one* when we speak nu-
> "'merically, and wish to signify that there are
> "'not more than one; whereas we use either *a*
> "'or *an* when we wish to emphasize not the
> "'*number* but the *description* of the thing spoken
> "'of.' What does he mean by speaking '*nume-*
> "'*rically*'?"

As Mr. S. evidently does not know the meaning
"of *numerically*", I refer him to '*Worcester's Ameri-*
'*can Dictionary*'; there he will find that it means
"*with respect to number*". The answer, then, to
Mr. S.'s question is very simple:—to "*speak*
"*numerically*" is to "*speak with respect to*
"*number*". Yet Mr. S. says;—"Mr. Moon's phrase
"absolutely means nothing. He might as well say
"that a man *speaks classically* because he speaks
"*with reference to the classics.*" The summing
up of this beautiful specimen of collegiate logic
may be made thus:—Because "*classically*" means
in a classical manner, "*numerically*" must mean
in a numerical manner; and because "*classi-*
"*cally*" does not mean with respect to the

classics, "*numerically*" cannot mean with respect to number! If Mr. S. allows himself to be led away by that "*Will-o'-the-wisp*", the analogous construction of words, he will find himself and his pupils struggling in a bog of absurdities. For instance, let him take the English words "*wick*" and "*wicked*", and the corresponding French words "*mèche*" and "*méchant*", and he will be able to prove, if not to the satisfaction of scholars, at least to his own satisfaction, that there is an intimate relationship between a man and a tallow candle!

CRITICISM XII.

THE HON. GEORGE P. MARSH.

CONDENSATION is one of the last lessons which a young writer learns. He is afraid to be simple, and has no faith in beauty which is unadorned; hence, he crowds his sentences with superlatives, and never uses a noun without accompanying it with an adjective. In his estimation, turgidity passes for eloquence, and simplicity is but an other name for that which is weak and unmeaning. But there is an error which is the very opposite of diffuseness, and which is equally to be avoided. It consists of so injudicious a compression of our language that the meaning becomes distorted. I will illustrate this by the following passage from Mr. Marsh's '*Notes*'. He says;—

> "Not only every author known to fame, but hundreds
> "whose names have scarcely survived themselves,
> "have been, or will be, carefully read, and every
> "first occurrence, every happy use, every forcible
> "example of each word, accepted for introduction
> "into the dictionary."

The errors in this sentence are obvious. *"Every"* is singular; whereas *"all"* is either singular or plural; therefore, as the verb is in the plural, it would have been better to say;— "Not only *all authors* known to fame, but hun-"dreds whose names have scarcely survived "themselves *have been,*" etc. In the latter part of the sentence, where it may be thought undesirable to change *"every"* into *"all"*, the verb should have been put in the singular, thus :— "*Every* first occurrence, *every* happy use, *every* "forcible example *has been,* or will be, accepted".

Mr. Marsh's sentence is singularly faulty. What are we to understand by "every first "occurrence......of each word"? How can there be more than one *first* occurrence of each word?

There is, in '*Booth's Principles of English* '*Grammar*',* page 115, an excellent rule respecting the proper use of

"*shall*" and "*will*".

It is as follows :—"If the speaker is the nomi-"native to the verb, and also determines its

* "Booth certainly excelled most other grammarians in learning and acuteness."—*G. Brown's 'Grammar of English Grammars,*' p. 233.

"accomplishment;—or, if he is neither the
"nominative to the verb nor determines its
"accomplishment, — the proper auxiliary is
"'*will*': in every other case it is '*shall*'."
Let the reader follow me in illustrating this
rule, and its value will soon be apparent to
him. I will take the old story of the man
who fell into the water and exclaimed;—"I *will*
"be drowned, and nobody *shall* save me." In
the phrase "I will be drowned", the speaker
is the nominative to the verb, but he did not
mean to determine its accomplishment; he had
no intention of being drowned; hence, the impropriety of his using "*will*". In the phrase "no-
"body shall save me", the speaker was not the
nominative to the verb, neither did he intend to
determine its accomplishment; therefore he
could not with propriety use "*shall*". He should
have said;—I *shall* be drowned, and nobody *will*
"save me"; because, in the first clause, the
speaker is the nominative to the verb, but does
not determine its accomplishment; hence, the
propriety of using "*shall*"; and, in the last
clause, he is neither the nominative to the verb,
nor does he determine its accomplishment; hence,
the propriety of using "*will*". Mr. Marsh, in

speaking of the English lexicon now in process of compilation by the London Philological Society, says ;—

> " But though we have thus held ourselves aloof from
> " this great enterprise, the orthography which
> " *shall* be adopted by the editors of this lexicon
> " will, probably, be universally accepted on our
> " side of the Atlantic as well as on the other."

By the foregoing rule, we see that Mr. Marsh should have used " *will* " instead of " *shall* ".

There are some words which, describing a condition that is unalterable, do not admit of comparison. One of these is " *universal*"; yet what is more common than to read of a practice which is said to be "*so* universal"? Another of these words is "*perfect*"; yet writers are continually speaking of " a *more perfect* " state of things. What is meant, we can only guess. " *Complete* " is another word of this class. The idea which it conveys is that of a state of fulness, having no deficiency, entire. What, then, does Mr. Marsh wish us to understand by

> " *Completest*", " our *completest* dictionaries ", "*greater*
> " completeness " ?

How can anything be *completer* than that which
is *complete?*   How can there be a *better* than
the *best,* or a *greater* than the *greatest?*   One
dictionary may be more copious, or be more
comprehensive, than an other ; but it cannot be
more *complete;* for, completeness is a fixed state,
one not admitting of increase.   I am aware that
the Most High has been spoken of as the Most
Highest ; and the solecism has been pardoned
in consideration of the intensity of the religious
feeling in which it had its origin.   I am aware,
also, that Milton has spoken of a depth which is
"*lower*" than the "*lowest*".   But, whatever
license may be allowed to a great poet, such an
expression in simple prose is sheer nonsense.

There is a nice distinction to be observed between the meaning of the words

"*so*" and "*as*"

when used in connection with such superlative
words as those of which I have been speaking.
We may say of two things, each of which is perfect ;—" one is *as perfect* as the other"; but if we
wish to speak in a negative form and to state of
two things, that one is perfect and the other is
not perfect, however near it may be to perfection,

we cannot say;—" one is not *so perfect* as the
" other "; and the reason why it cannot be said
is, that the expression implies the existence of
degrees of perfection; or, in other words, that a
thing can be perfect and not perfect at the same
time. . "*So* perfect", "*so* supreme", "*so* univer-
"sal", are all wrong: a thing cannot be partly
supreme or partly universal. A whole contains
its parts; but a part cannot contain the whole,
and therefore ought not to be spoken of by a
term which is applicable only to the whole. It
will be seen, then, that "*so*" and "*as*" are not
interchangeable.

Booth says, on page 80;—"In comparative
"clauses of equality, '*as*' is both the relative
"and the antecedent; *e.g.*—'John is ' *as* brave
"*as* James.' But when one of the parts differs
"from the other in degree, the antecedent is
"'*so*';—'John is *not so* brave *as* James.' The
"general rule is that '*as*' alludes to likeness and
"similarity, while '*so*' refers to the comparison .
"of extent or degree, and it is in the misappre-
"hension of this English idiom that the natives
"of Scotland are so apt to err. 'I will answer
"'his letter *so* soon *as* I receive it', should be
"written '*as* soon *as*', because the point of time

"is the same. 'He is not *as* rich *as* he was',
"should be '*so* rich *as*', etc., because the states
"are unequal. 'He ran *as* fast *as* I did', is
"equality. 'He ran *so* fast *that* I could not
"' overtake him ', is superiority. '*As* great', '*as*
"' much', '*as* high', is a *bulk, quantity,* and
"*height* exactly equal to something to which the
"'*as*' relates; but '*so* great', '*so* much', '*so*
"' high ', is a certain degree of *bulk, quantity,* and
"*height,* which requires to be ascertained by a
"comparison of *less* or *more.*"

Mr. Marsh says;—

"In a lexicon of a dead language the vocabulary of
"the recorded literature may be absolutely com-
"plete *so* far *as* the specification of the words
"which composed it is concerned."

From the foregoing remarks, the reader will at
once perceive that Mr. Marsh ought to have
"said;—*as* far *as* the specification of the words
"which composed it is concerned."

Nothing in Mr. Marsh's '*Notes*' so much sur-
prises me as his misuse of words. Here is an other
instance. He speaks of

"A scientific vocabulary of not *less* than 300,000
"words."

Is it really necessary to remind Mr. Marsh that

"*less*" refers to quantity in *bulk*, and that "*fewer*" is the proper word to use when speaking of *numbers?*

Mr. Marsh says ;—

"Such persons are apt to fancy that they detect, or "rather [,] feel, an inherent significance in the "words of their native speech. In their view "a house is called *house* because it *is* a house : a "horse is called *horse* because it *is* a horse. To "them the name is as truly and as obviously a "quality or property of the animal as his color "or the number of *his legs,* and *they* often mani- "fest a virtuous indignation against the unhappy "foreigner who knows no better than to call a "horse a *cheval.*"

Concerning this passage I have one question to ask :—Is the virtuous indignation against the luckless foreigner, manifested by the horse's legs ?

One more question :—On what do Flemish painters live—what is their food ? Mr. Marsh is surely joking when he speaks of—

"The battered copper vessels, old brooms, cobwebs, "appleparings, and the like, which the Flemish "painters scatter so freely about *their interiors.*"

When a word which has a technical, as well as a literal, signification is used technically, it should be enclosed in inverted commas.

CRITICISM XIII.

THE HON. GEORGE P. MARSH.

A KNOWLEDGE of grammar may be acquired by study; but by no amount of study can a man who is destitute of good taste acquire that delicate quality of mind; though it is as essential to gracefulness of expression in language, as are a musical ear and soul, to the *true* utterances of the musician and of the poet.

What are we to think of a verbal critic who uses a noun in three totally different senses in one criticism; and who, as if that were not enough, then makes confusion more confounded, by prefixing to the noun, when next he uses it, such an adjective, that his description of a term in grammar is identical with a storekeeper's hackneyed description of his wares? I speak of facts. The Hon. George P. Marsh's champion, Mr. S., of Trinity College, (for I have not yet finished with him,) tells us not only of an "*article*" [a criticism] upon the "*article*" [*a* or *an*] ; but, after mentioning grocers and druggists and their "*articles*" [of commerce], speaks of the little word "*an*" as "*a genuine article*"!

"Can such things be . . . without our special wonder ?"

The following is an other specimen of Mr. S.'s tautology. He says ;—

> "I come now to a *sentence* which is one of Mr. Moon's "most characteristic *sentences;* perhaps, also, it "is one of his most erroneous *sentences:* 'It is "'a curious fact, mentioned in a recent number "'of the '*Athenæum*', that we English alone of "'all nations, ancient or modern, have a *bonâ* "'*fide* article which is distinct from '*one*', though "'contracted from '*one*', and meaning '*one*'.'"

The foregoing, which Mr. S. calls one of my most characteristic sentences, is really not mine ; it is a literal quotation from the '*Athenæum* , No. 1929, page 497, and ought to have been marked as such by inverted commas. However, as the commas have been omitted, and, consequently, the sentence stands as if it were mine, I will examine Mr. S.'s condemnation of it. He states, in the first place, that—

> "The whole assertion is untrue, because the Ameri- "can nation has the same article as the English

"nation, and therefore the English nation does
"not stand *alone* in this respect."

This is another instance of S.'s limited knowledge of the meaning of words. Evidently, he
thinks that the word *"nation"* is synonymous
with *"people"*; but it is not; and that the
writer in the *'Athenæum'* is correct in his use of
the word, will be seen on reading the following
extract from *'Worcester's American Dictionary:*—
"Nation denotes a race of men, or connection by
"birth or descent; *people*, persons or men of
"common subordination, or those who form a
"community. The *people* of Saxony and Bavaria
"are a portion of the German *nation.*" When,
in discoursing on language we speak of "the
"English", or "the English nation", we include
all those *peoples* which are connected with us by
birth, or by descent, and who speak that language.
The Americans are not a part of the English
people; but they are, in the true sense of the
term, a part of the English *nation;* (L. *natio*,
from *nascor*, to be born) *i.e.*, a race of men connected with the English *by birth.*

Mr. S. next objects to the expression

"We English";

and says, of the word "*English*"; — "When
"it denotes the nation or people, it must be
"preceded by the definite article or by a de-
"monstrative pronoun." Surely, what is true
of the word "*English*", used in that sense, is true
also of the word "*Americans*"? Why, then,
does Mr. S. object to my saying,—"*We English*";
and yet allow himself to say,—"*We Americans*"?
His theory is justly condemned by his own practice in the very page containing his dogmatical
assertion respecting it. The expressions, "*We*
"*English*", "*We Americans*", "*O ye Corinthians*":
(2 Cor., vi, 11) are strictly correct. "*English*",
by itself, means the language; but "English",
with a personal pronoun before it, means *Englishmen.*
Of course, in elliptical expressions, "*English*"
may have various meanings.

The next objection raised by my collegiate
critic is to the expression "*alone of all nations*".
He says ;—

"'*Of all nations*' is properly used only in denoting a
   "comparison after a superlative, *e.g.*, the greatest
   "of all nations; or it is used after a numeral.
   "Mr. Moon uses it in neither of these two ways,
   "[it would have been sufficient, to say,—'*neither*
   "'*of these ways*'; the idea of there being '*two*',

"is conveyed in the word '*neither*,'] and therefore
"he misuses it. Would it not be better to say:
"alone *among* all nations?"

Mr. S. is still blundering over the use of the preposition "*of*"; not knowing that "one *of* them"
is "one *among* them". He says that the phrase
"*of all nations*" is properly used only in denoting
a comparison after a superlative, and that I have
not used it in that way. Indeed! I have always
thought that "*alone*" is a superlative. I suppose
that they say at Trinity College;—"*alone*",
"*aloner*", "*alonest*"! Mr. S. adds;—"or it is
"used after a numeral. Mr. Moon uses it in
"neither of these two ways". Mr. S. does not
seem to know the derivation of even the simple
word "*alone*"; let me, then, tell him that "*alone*"
is a contraction of "*all one*"; and if "*one*" is not
a numeral, will Mr. S. tell me what it is? Very
oddly, it happens that on the first page of the
number of '*The Nation*' containing these remarks of Mr. S.'s, there is the expression,
"Kansas, *alone of all the states*".

The phrase "*ancient or modern*" next comes
under Mr. S.'s condemnation. He says;—

"The conjunction '*or*' treacherously leads Mr. Moon
"into a singular error. He divides the nations

" into two classes, ancient nations and modern
" nations, and asserts that, in *either* of these
" classes, the English is the only nation which
" has a *bonâ fide* article. The English is the *only*
" *one of the ancient nations !* "

There is a subtile fallacy here which must be
exposed. The writer in ' *The Athenæum* ' does
not say that the English is one of the ancient
nations. He says that the English is one " *of*
" *all nations* ". He then divides the " *all nations*"
into two sections ; the one, " ancient " ; the other,
" modern " ; but that division does not make the
writer place the English among the ancient
nations *to the exclusion of the modern,* nor among
the modern nations *to the exclusion of the ancient.*
The English is still one " *of all nations* ". It is one
thing to say ;—" We English alone of all ancient
" nations or of all modern nations ", and it is
an other thing to say ;—" We English alone of
" all nations ancient or modern ". The former
expression divides the nations into two classes,
and places the English nation, first in one
class, and afterward in the other ; whereas the
latter expression places the English among
" *all nations* ", and *then* divides those nations
into two classes ; the one, " ancient " ; the other,

I

"modern". As for Mr. S.'s emendation;—
that of substituting "*and*" for "*or*", I should
much like to know how "*all nations*" can be
said to be "ancient *and* modern". Some are
ancient, and some are modern; therefore, they
may "*all*" be classed under the designation
'ancient *or* modern"; and this the writer in
'*The Athenæum*' has done. But they are not all
"ancient *and* modern". So that instead of the
conjunction "*or*" having treacherously led Mr.
Moon into a singular error, it is the conjunction
"*and*" which has treacherously led Mr. S. into
a singular error.

There are several other inaccuracies and misstatements in Mr. S.'s letter, but my patience
fails me; so, after one more exposure of my
opponent's errors, I will finish this criticism. He
censures me for saying

"the using it",

and supports his opinion by the following quotation from Lindley Murray:—"The present
"participle, with the definite article '*the*' before
"it, becomes a substantive, and *must* have the
"preposition '*of*' after it." Let us examine this.
Supposing I were speaking of my having had the
good fortune to meet two of my old school-fellows,

Edwin and Arthur; I should manifest very great
ignorance of the proprieties of language if, following the rule quoted by Mr. S., I were to speak of
the meeting as, "the meeting *of* Edwin and
Arthur." That would be to describe their meeting
each other, not my meeting them. The case may
be very simply put thus: the act was, *meeting
Edwin and Arthur;* the agent was, *myself;* the
act, therefore, was *my act;* consequently, *my
act* was "*my meeting Edwin and Arthur*"; and
"*my meeting*" was "*the meeting which took place*".
Now, according to Lindley Murray's rule, as
quoted by his devoted disciple, Mr. S., of Trinity
College, I ought to say that it was "the meeting
of which took place"! because "*meeting*" is the
present participle of the verb "*to meet*"; and,
being preceded by the definite article "*the*", becomes a substantive, and "*must* have the prepo-
"sition '*of*' after it." Mr. S.'s conversation
must be singularly puzzling. I can imagine
him saying to his college friends;—"The prepar-
"ing *of* [for] my departure, the driving *of* [to]
"the station, the entering *of* [upon] the railway
"journey, and the arriving *of* [at] my destina-
"tion, seem now like a dream."

Finally, if I say of this rule;—"the making

I 2

"*of* it is a disgrace to Lindley Murray", my words refer to the *manner* in which it has been made; but if I say;—"*the making it* is a "disgrace to Lindley Murray", my words very properly refer, not to the mode of the action, but to the action itself.

As Mr. S. has written to me "for the last "time", and has kindly bid me good-by, I return the valediction, and at the same time thank him for his courtesy. Although I differ with him on many points, I acknowledge that I have profited by his criticisms. "*He who wrestles with us,* "*strengthens us; our antagonist is thus our* "*helper.*"—BURKE.

THIRD PART.

CRITICISMS,

ORIGINALLY PUBLISHED IN AMERICA,

ON

EDWARD S. GOULD'S "GOOD ENGLISH".

BAD ENGLISH EXPOSED.

CRITICISM XIV.

EDWARD S. GOULD.

In Mr. Gould's '*Good English*' there is much to be commended; much for which we owe him our thanks. His reprobation of errors, common to the current literature of the day, is timely and valuable; but far more so is the evidence which he brings forward, that even our most careful writers are sometimes off their guard—himself among the number.

I at first shrank from exposing Mr. Gould's errors; and that, partly for my own sake and partly for his: for *my own* sake, because I feared that it would be considered discourteous to do so, after his laudatory remarks on ' *The Dean's* ' *English* '; and for *his* sake, because adverse criticism might injuriously affect his reputation as an author; and he really has done good service in the field of letters, and merits praise rather than reproof. But the very ability displayed in his work, magnifies the gravity of the errors which it contains; hence, the need of a public protest against them. Under these circumstances, Mr. Gould will, I trust, while he accepts the criticisms themselves as a mild rebuke for his carelessness, accept also the fact of my writing them, as an acknowledgment of much that is excellent in his work.

That hastily-written contributions to journals contain errors in grammar, and are faulty in construction, is not to be wondered at; but that there should be, in treatises on those errors, the identical faults which those treatises are written to condemn, is a circumstance well calculated to impress all students of the language, with the necessity for increased vigilance; for, if those who have specially devoted their time to the cultivation of a pure and an accurate style of writing, occasionally fail to write correctly, even after their most careful efforts, how numerous must be the faults of those who consider that but little attention on their part is needed, to perfect themselves in the knowledge and use of their mother tongue.

As a lesson, then, which may be instructive to such persons; and as an example of the proneness to error observable in the works of even those who aspire to the office of public teachers of grammar, let us look at the composition of Mr. Gould's *Good English, or Popular Errors in 'Language.'*

The very title implies an assurance that the author has taken great pains with the book; and this assurance is confirmed by our finding in it the following passages. I quote from page 61 :—

> "It is not overstating the case to say that Dean
> "Trench, while he is beyond question a writer of
> "general excellence and force, is frequently guilty
> "of extreme carelessness,—*which, in books of phi-*
> "*lological criticism, is hardly to be excused.*"

Again, page 116 :—

> "The Dean [of Canterbury] can plead neither haste
> "nor inadvertence in his present work; ....
> "*he may fairly be held responsible for every error*
> "*it contains.*"

Once more, page 131:—

> "And now, as to the style of the Dean's book, taken
> "as a whole. He must be held responsible for
> "every error in it; *because, as has been shown, he*
> *has had full leisure for its revision.*"

Surely, such language is not more applicable to Archbishop Trench and to Dean Alford, than it is to him who critically reviews their writings; and I beg that the readers of the following criticisms will bear in mind what Mr. E. S. Gould has said upon this subject, and they will see how gladly at last he shelters himself behind the very defence which he denied to others.

There are, in Mr. Gould's book, instances of erroneous judgment, as well as errors of grammar. One of the former occurs in reference to a passage of mine in a criticism on Mr. Marsh's essays. I had said;—

> "That, no doubt, *was* what he intended to do; but
> " certainly it *was* not what he did."

Concerning this, Mr. Gould remarks that the italicized words should be in the present tense, and not in the past, as I have put them. With all due respect to Mr. Gould's opinion in general, I beg leave to differ with him here. In expressing either abstract or universal truths, the present tense of the verb ought undoubtedly to be employed; and if a circumstance spoken of exists only in the present, then, too, the verb must be in the present tense; but if we

are speaking not of abstract truths, but of
some specific circumstance which existed in the
past and which still exists, we may, at our
option, speak of either its past or its present
state. In the criticism referred to, that which
the person spoken of intended to do, and that
which he did not intend to do, are as much
matters of the past, as they are of the present;
therefore, my sentence is not incorrect; I say,
"*is* not"; but if I chose to speak of the past, I
might say that it "*was* not" incorrect. A
very simple test of the fitness or of the unfitness
of the tense of the verb to convey our meaning
is, to put the adverb "*now*" after the verb in
the present tense, and the adverb "*then*" after
the verb in the past tense.

Mr. Gould has done well to notice the common
error of confounding the past and present tenses
of verbs; but an apter illustration of it may be
found in a sentence of his own. On page 186,
he says of Kean and Macready;—

> "And the result *was*, that they gained the prize for
> "which they contended; namely, enduring fame."

Now, the perpetuity of Kean's and of Macready's
fame, is a matter of the present and of the

future, rather than of the past; indeed, if the
fame existed in the past only, it could not properly be said to be "*enduring*".   Therefore, it
would be more consistent to say;—"The result
"*is* that they have gained enduring fame."

Elsewhere Mr. Gould censures me for not
exposing what he calls an error of Dean Alford's;
but it is Mr. Gould who is in fault in condemning Dean Alford for what is not an error, and me
for not exposing it.   The passage in question is
this:—"If I had believed the Queen's English to
"*have been* rightly laid down by the dictionaries
"and the professors of rhetoric, I need not have
"troubled myself to write about it."   Mr. Gould
says that this is wrong; and that the Dean
should have said;—"If I had believed it to *be*",
etc.   In my opinion both forms are right; and
Mr. Gould errs in condemning either of them.

An other instance is found on page 191.   I
read:—

> "It is needless for me to add, that your doing so
> "*would* [*future*] cost you no effort.   You would
> "merely *have done* [*past*] what you do every
> "day, without a thought as to how you do it."

It seems as if Mr. Gould had here sacrificed

grammatical propriety, for the sake of avoiding too frequent a repetition of the little word *"do"*. He makes matters worse. Why did he not reconstruct his sentence ?

There is, on page 28, an other example of this kind of error ; but it is an error in exactly the opposite direction :—the present tense is there used instead of the past, not the past instead of the present. It is in some otherwise sensible remarks concerning the use of the words *"beside"* and *"besides"*. Mr. Gould says ;—

> " Our lexicographers *have contented* themselves with
> "leaving these two words as they *find* them in
> "the pages of good and bad writers—jumbled
> "together without any attempt at discrimination
> "between them."

The expression *"our lexicographers"* must, unquestionably, include Johnson, Walker, Rich-ardson, Webster, and others, who are dead; how, then, can they be said to *"find"* those two words in the pages of good and bad writers ? Surely there is not, in the next world, any reading of the works of bad writers, whatever there may be of those of good ones ! Mr. Gould should have said ;—" Our lexicographers contented "themselves with leaving these two words as

"they *found* them in the pages of good and *of*
"bad writers." The preposition "*of*" is needed
here, because the writers mentioned are, evidently, not those uncertain writers who sometimes write well and sometimes ill; but two
distinct classes of writers; the one, good; the
other, bad.

In commenting on the vulgarism of using the
word "*figure*" for "*number*", Mr. Gould brings
forward a passage from Dean Alford's '*Queen's
English*', where the vulgarism is found, and he
adds ;—

"*Mem*. Put *that* against some of the Dean's sneers!"

If the Dean should happen to read Mr. Gould's
work, he will find that the passage begins
thus :—

"Newspaper usage and oral usage has [they has !]
"made this word synonymous with *amount*";

and I fancy that the Dean will say with a
smile ;—"*Mem*. Put *that* against some of *Mr*.
"*Gould's* sneers !"

Should the Dean continue his perusal of the
book, he will, doubtless, wince under Mr. Gould's
sarcasm, on page 133 :—"Neither of which *are*

"taken into account", says the Dean.   "Com-
"ment here is needless", remarks Mr. Gould.
But, on page 197, the Dean has his revenge; for
Mr. Gould says;—

> " He may have studied his way by the chart, and may
> " think that he has mastered its sinuosities; but
> " *the misleading power* of the verse divisions—
> " which seem to be guides and are not—constantly
> " *betray* [it betray !] him into difficulty."

Mr. Gould has forgotten that the nominative
to his verb is in the singular.

These *singular* mistakes are really astonishing!
How are they to be avoided ?   Only by the cultivation of a habit of careful patient examination
of the diversity of meaning produced by the
different placing of the same words.   As one
means to that end, I strongly urge all students
of the language to acquire a practical knowledge
of the game of chess.   It tends to produce
precision of mind ; and, by accustoming the
player to weigh well the relative position and
influence of every piece on the board, makes more
familiar and easy to him the task of judging
accurately concerning the position and influence
of every word in a sentence.

CRITICISM XV.

EDWARD S. GOULD.

THERE is a puzzling inconsistency in Mr. Gould's use of certain phrases.   On page 213, he says ;—

> "The majority *remain*" ;

again, on page 166, he says ;—

> "The majority *speak* in favour of the great changes "that have been made";

but, on page 42, he says ;—

> "The majority *has* the best of the argument."

If "*majority*" is used as a noun in the plural in one place, why is it used as a noun in the singular in an other?   Moreover, in the very paragraph in which "*majority*" is used as a noun in the singular, (page 42,) "*minority*" is used as a noun in the plural :—

" The opposing minority *become* mere schismatics."

Then, on the opposite page, we are taken back
to the singular :—

" The number *makes* but a very small minority ";

and, on page 73, we return to the plural :—

" An abundance of followers *were* found ".

An abundance *were !*

I do not know whether the use of " *shall*" and
" *will*" is different in the United States from
what it is in England ; but the same peculiarity
respecting its use is observable in the writings of
the Hon. George P. Marsh, Dr. M. Schele De Vere,
and Mr. Gould. Each of these writers occasionally
uses either " *will*" or " *would*" where an English-
man would use either " *shall*" or " *should*".
Mr. Gould says, on page 212, and, again, on
page 222 ;—" *I would like* " to do so-and-so.
On this side of the Atlantic we call such an
expression a Scotticism. Certainly it is not pure
English.

It seems strange that Mr. Gould should have
forgotten the rule that not only do conjunctions
couple like moods and cases, but that, " in

"general, any two terms which we connect by a
"conjunction should be the same in kind or
"quality rather than different or heterogeneous".
On pages 29 and 30 I read as follows;—

> "They are reproduced here for the twofold purpose
> "*of relieving* the writer of this book from a
> "suspicion of plagiarism; and *to show* that his
> "views, as then expressed, are so far corrobo-
> "rated."

Mr. Gould having said, in the former clause
of the sentence;—"*of relieving*", should have
said, in the latter clause;—"*and of showing*".

Here is another sentence which is not properly
balanced; page 200 :—

> "But there is a large class of clergymen who know
> "the difficulty *of making* themselves heard, with-
> "out knowing the right method *to overcome* it."

This should be;—"the difficulty *of making*";
and, "the right method *of overcoming*".

On page 41, I read;—

> "In addition to *the misuse of* 'either' and 'neither'
> "these words are both frequently *mispro-*
> "*nounced.*"

This should be;—"In addition to *the misuse*

" of ' either' and ' neither' is *the frequent mispro-*
"*nunciation* of both these words."   The careful
reader of these criticisms will not have failed to
observe that I have altered the position of the
word "*both*".   This has been done to bring the
sentence into strict accordance with the meaning
which Mr. Gould intended to convey.   He did
not intend to speak of words which are "*both*
"*frequently mispronounced*" and frequently something else ; but to speak of "*both words*" as being
frequently mispronounced.   Hence, the necessity
for the alteration.   The parts of a sentence
which are most closely connected in meaning
should be as closely as possible connected in
position.

As for adverbs, Mr. Gould censures Archbishop
Trench for having, in ' *English Past and Present*',
misplaced the adverb "*only*", and said ;—"*only*
"*different*", when he ought to have said ;—
"*different only* "; yet Mr. Gould himself, on the
very next page, (61,) similarly errs in using the
adverb "*also*"; and writes ;—

" *Trench also* says, in the same volume," etc. ;

as if ' *English   Past   and   Present*' had not been
written by him solely !   What Mr. Gould means

is ;—" Trench says also, in the same volume,"
etc.

On page 105, Mr. Gould gives us a list of
words ending in " *logy*", and says ;—

> " Of these, one *only takes* ' er ' as an exclusive termi-
> "nation, namely, 'astrologer '."

Why does Mr. Gould censure Archbishop Trench
for saying " *only different*", and yet himself say
" *only takes*"?　　He should have said ;—" Of
"these, *only one* takes ' er' as an exclusive
"termination, namely, ' *astrologer'*."　　Of course,
in some sentences the expressions " *only different*"
and " *only takes*" would be correct.　　The position
which the adverb must occupy is determined by
the meaning of the writer.

There is a similar error on page 150.　Mr.
Gould there says ;—

> " In *Webster's Dictionary* of 1866, the following words
> "are retained in their exclusiveness, that is,
> "they are not *severally united* by brackets with
> " orthodox orthography."

If I were disposed to be hypercritical, I might
ask, what the apparently self-contradictory expression, " *severally united*", means ; and also,

what kind of things "*brackets with orthodox
"*orthography*" are. But, seriously, Mr. Gould
ought to have said;—"*they, severally,* are not
"united by brackets to the same words spelt
" according to orthodox orthography."

Mr. Gould tells us, on page 50, that "ad-
"verbs refer to, or qualify, what a person or
"thing *does;* and adjectives, what a person or
"thing *is,* or *seems* to be." As he evidently is
familiar with the rule respecting the proper use
of adverbs and of adjectives, I am surprised
to find him saying, on page 204;—

> "This passage is more commonly read *wrong* than,
> "perhaps, any other in the Bible."

Is not reading an act—a something which a
person "*does*"? Why, then, does not Mr. Gould
qualify it by the adverb "*wrongly*"?

Mr. Gould finds fault with Dean Alford for
saying "*more decisive*", and asks, on page 112;—

> "Does the Dean hold that *decisive* is an adjective
> "that admits of comparison?"

I reply, on behalf of my former antagonist, by
asking Mr. Gould whether "*universally*" and
"*totally*" admit of comparison? If not, why does

he condemn the Dean for saying "*more decisive*"
and yet himself say, on page 38;—"the phrase is
"now *so universally* used"; and, on page 178,
say;—"*so totally* at variance with well-estab-
"lished conclusions"?   A *decision*, of a court of
law, for instance, may be confirmed by a higher
tribunal, and thereby be made "*more decisive*";
but "*universality*" and "*totality*" cannot be otherwise than perfect or complete.   To use language
implying that anything can be universal, and
yet only partly universal; or total, and yet only
partly total, is to speak nonsensically; yet such
is the import of Mr. Gould's expressions, "*so*
"universally", "*so* totally".   The little word
"*so*" is often misused in Mr. Gould's '*Good*
'*English*'.   It occurs four times in four consecutive lines, on page 213.   I there read;—

> " Cannot see why the clergyman should be *so*.   But
> "for all that he is *so;* it is in the nature of
> "things that he should be *so;* and he is nearly
> "helpless while he remains *so*."

This is the very opposite of elegant.
"*So*" and "*such*" are very greatly in favour
with demonstrative young ladies; with them,
every beautiful object is either "*such* a beauty!"

or "*so* beautiful!" The *excessive* use of these words, or, indeed, of any set form of words, is a mannerism, and should be avoided. "*So*", in its proper place, is a very precious little word; and no where is it more precious than in the expression;—"God *so* loved the world". But the "*so*", in Mr. Gould's expression—"*so* to-"tally", destroys the force of the word which it is meant to intensify.

Of the phrase "*in so far as*", Mr. Gould says, on page 62;—

> "It seems strange that *so* clumsy a phrase could get
> "into use when the proper phrase is *so* familiar
> "and simple; but *so* it is that men will cumber
> "themselves about [*with*] many things when but
> "few things are needed. The *in* of the phrase is
> "worse than superfluous."

Now turn to page 166, and you will find Mr. Gould writing as follows :—

> "The work as it now stands *and* with the exceptions
> "*herein-above* designated, is worthy of the praise
> "bestowed on it; for its entire reconstuction
> "has made it what it should be,—always except-
> "ing the uneradicated tares of Webster's sow-
> "ing."

If Mr. Gould will apply the reasoning that is

found on page 62 of his work, to the language
on page 166 of it, he will strike out the "*and*"
and the "*herein*", for they, too, are "*worse than*
"*superfluous*."

"*So*" is most frequently misused when in connection with "*as*". Whether Mr. Gould is
speaking affirmatively, or negatively, he almost
always says;—"*so—as*",—rarely, if ever, "*as—*
"*as*"; yet, in comparative clauses of *equality*,
the latter expression is the correct one ; and the
former, the correct one in comparative clauses
of *inequality*. Having, in a previous criticism,
fully discussed this matter, it is not necessary
here to do more than show in what way Mr.
Gould has misused the words. I read as
follows :—

Page 21.—"*so* long as its place is occupied ".
  „   37.—*so* far, at least, as the dictionary is con-
             "cerned ".
  „   94.—"This is very well, *so* far as it goes ".
  „   115.—"This is fortunate, *so* far as its author is
             "correct ".
  „   121.—"*so* far as the newspapers are concerned ".
  „   143.—"And *so* long as he occupies the secretary's
             "desk ".
  „   159.—"it is to be observed that, *so* far as we
             "know ".
  „   191.—"*so* far as that sentence is concerned ".

Page 214.—"*so* far as I can".

„   217.—"he should ...... *so* far as he can".

„   223.—"*so* far as I can judge".

In each of these passages, "*so*" should be changed for "*as*". The only sentences which I can call to mind, where the words "*so—as*" are proper when speaking affirmatively, are those in which the last of the said words precedes a verb in the infinitive mood, *e.g.*:— "An author should *so* write *as to be* clearly "understood"; and those in which we use the words *emphatically*. For instance:—"How can "you descend to a thing *so* base *as* falsehood?"

CRITICISM XVI.

EDWARD S. GOULD.

HAVING, in the two previous letters, examined the grammatical composition of Mr. Gould's work, and incidentally glanced at his condemnation of certain expressions of Archbishop Trench's and of Dean Alford's, I purpose now to consider Mr. Gould's choice of words and their relative positions in his sentences, in the work under review.

He speaks strongly against Noah Webster for his attempted alterations in the orthography of the language; and, in Mr. Gould's denunciation of the learned lexicographer, he so far lets his indignation get the mastery over him, that it carries him away beyond the bounds of prudence. With an exuberance of metaphor, which gives evidence of the fertility of his imagination, rather than of the soundness of his judgment, he describes Dr. Webster as an *alchemist;* moreover, as an *alchemist* engaged in *"tinkering"!*—the said *"tinkering"* is declared to have the effect of imparting a lesson in *husbandry!* while the general result of his labours is designated, *"the "progress of the plague"!*   Surely, Mr. Gould must have been trying to emulate the Irishman who, at a public meeting, rose in a state of great excitement, and said ;—" Gentlemen, the apple " of discord has been thrown into our midst; " and if it be not nipped in the bud, it will burst " into a conflagration which will deluge the " world !"

The passage to which I refer occurs on page 165, and reads thus :—

> "The fact remains, that all [that] Webster really
> " accomplished by his *alchemy,* is a hopeless
> " confusion [how can a man *accomplish* a con-
> " fusion?] in the spelling of (derivatives and all)
> " [" *and all* " what?] perhaps two hundred words
> " in a dictionary that contains nearly a hundred
> " thousand words. Whereas, before Webster com-
> " menced his *tinkering,* the spelling of those two
> " hundred words, however irregular to his appre-
> " hension, was more uniform than probably it ever
> " will be again.   He has proved how much easier
> " it is to *sow tares* than to root them out.   .   .
> " After the concessions made in the quarto of
> " 1866, there is some hope that the further *pro-
> " gress of the plague* may be stayed."

In the introduction of Mr. Gould's book there occurs the following passage :—

"His word was spurious originally, and he cannot
"remove its taint, nor can any subsequent en-
"dorsement purify it."

Mr. Gould had been speaking of a *word* under
the similitude of a *counterfeit coin; (vide seq.),* his
appellation of "*spurious*" is, therefore, correct;
but, to speak of its being *tainted,* is, I think, rather
a perversion of terms; and when he further speaks
of its being *purified by an endorsement,* I am lost
in wonder how any person, writing on the subject
of '*Good English*', could so forget the proprieties
of language as to use words which are but little
calculated to convey his meaning.

Mr. Gould tells us, on page 4, that—

"The pages of our best writers are thickly *sprinkled*
"*with violations* of the plainest grammatical
"rules."

Assuredly his use of figurative language is in
frequent violation of the plain and simple rule
that all "*figure*" should be appropriate.

He condemns the use of the word "*couple*",
except when it refers to two things *coupled
together.* I do not object to that; but I do object

to his use of the word *"entire"* when speaking
of *number.* He says, on page 22 ;—

" The *entire* number ";

this should be,—" The *total* number". *Entire*
has reference to that which is unbroken ; *whole,*
to that of which no part is wanting. *Total* is
the proper word to use in speaking of the aggregate of numbers.

Again, on page 41, the word *"less"*, which is an
adjective of *quantity in bulk,* is employed as a
synonym for *"fewer"*, which is an adjective of
quantity in number. He says ;—

" No *less* than *five* ".

The same error occurs on page 44 :—

" No *less* than *three* ".

Mr. Gould should have said ;—"no *fewer* than
" five";—" no *fewer* than three ".

In condemning the phrase,—" *looked beauti-*
"*fully* ", Mr. Gould says ;—

" *A deal* of argument has been expended on the
" question ".

He might, perhaps, think that I were jesting if

I asked him whether he meant *a little deal,* or *a great deal.* The former expression, very strangely, is never used; but the commonness of the latter expression might have taught Mr. Gould that "*deal*" means merely "a portion or part". It is the German "*theil*", and is *indefinite as to quantity.* "*A deal* of argument" is "a portion "of argument"; it may be little, or it may be much.

"*Traced*" is a word that is misapplied by Mr. Gould. He says;—

> "Quaintness must not take the place of accuracy "in language: besides, though the phrase in "question may be *traced* to the Bible, it cannot "be found in the Bible."

I imagine Mr. Gould to mean that, though the phrase may be *imputed* to the Bible, it cannot be found there; for if it can be *traced*—its *track* be followed—to the Bible, it unquestionably can be found there.

Mr. Gould's use of "*relieve*" and "*knowingly*" next comes under consideration. On page 116, I read;—

> "The author deems it proper to say;— . . . that, "although from the Dean's statement, *passim,*

"in the '*Queen's English*, it seems that his book
"has been very frequently criticised in England,
"not a word of such criticism, [better, *that criti-*
"*cism;* 'such' means *similar*, but not *identical*]
"except such as [better, *except that which*] the
"Dean himself quotes, has ever been seen by the
"present writer;—a statement [tautology—Mr.
"Gould had just spoken of '*the Dean's statement*']
"which must relieve [*exonerate*] him from the
"charge of having knowingly ['wittingly' would
"have been a better word to use here; *knowingly*
"may mean *cunningly*] gone over the same ground
"as the English critics."

Further on, I read ;—

" A proper *estimate* of the value of these conflicting
"statements will presently be *undertaken.*"

We undertake "*to estimate*", "*to form an esti-*
"*mate*", "*to give an estimate*", or "*to make*
"*an estimate*"; but we do not undertake "*an*
"*estimate*".

The use of "*some*", for "*about*", is a very
common error.   It is found on page 186 of Mr.
Gould's work; he there says ;—

"The individual parts sustained by the actor do not
"contain more than *some* six hundred lines
"each."

On page 199, I read ;—

> "One thing more remains to be *said* on this subject,—
> "namely, a *suggestion* on the injury to the
> "voice."

A "*suggestion*" is a thing to be *made*, not
"*said*".

Lower down on the same page I find the
following passage :—

> "The next point to which I would call your atten-
> "tion is *audibleness;* a matter, in one respect,
> "more important than any *other principle* of
> "elocution."

Audibleness is an *essential* of elocution, but it
is not a *principle*.

Concerning a sentence of Archbishop Trench's,
Mr. Gould remarks, on page 110, that;—"he
"has, in the preceding sentence, so placed the
"words '*I think*', as to leave the reader in doubt
"whether they relate to what immediately pre-
"cedes [tautology—see '*preceding*' just above] or
"to what follows them."   But, on page 46, Mr.
Gould himself has written what is equally ambiguous, and that, too, from the very same cause.
He says ;—

" *Our Mutual Friend.* This is, so to speak, one of
 "the approved vulgarisms of the day; and, not-
 "withstanding the numberless exposures of its
 "vulgarity, *in newspapers, reviews, and elsewhere,*
 "it continues to flourish."

Do the italicized words refer to what precedes
them, or what follows them ? Is the *vulgarity*
of the *vulgarism* (I quote Mr. Gould's own words)
exposed " *in newspapers, reviews, and elsewhere* ";
or does he say of the vulgarism, that, "*in news-*
"*papers, reviews, and elsewhere, it continues to*
"*flourish* " ? I challenge the reader to come to
any definite conclusion on the subject.

One cannot but smile at some of Mr. Gould's
errors ; they are so ingeniously droll. He says,
on page 105 ;—

"There is no short single English word that performs
 "the duty of ' *lying* '."

Again ; observe the strange meaning given to
the following passage by the use of the pronoun
" *them* ", instead of the noun to which it is intended to refer. Mr. Gould says, on page 11 ;—

"Reference was made, in the introductory chapter, to
 "words fabricated by ignorant people, and after-
 "ward adopted by people of education. There

L

"are not many of *them* [? 'people of education'],
"speaking comparatively; but their number is
"every day increasing, and if their increase
"cannot be checked, they will soon be 'like the
"'stars for multitude'"!

Ambiguity in the use of pronouns cannot
always be avoided, and Dr. Campbell justly says
in his '*Philosophy of Rhetoric*', Vol. II, page
64;—"Some have imagined, that the pronoun
"ought always regularly to refer to the nearest
"preceding noun of the same gender and number.
"But this notion is founded in a mistake, and
"doth not suit the idiom of any language,
"ancient or modern." With equal propriety,
however, the learned Doctor says, on page 55;—
"As the signification of the pronouns is ascer-
"tained merely by the antecedent to which they
"refer, *the greatest care must be taken, if we would
"express ourselves perspicuously, that the reference
"be unquestionable.*"

There are, in Mr. Gould's work, many other
passages which might be critically examined,
with advantage to the English student, but I
trust that I have said enough to show that it is
extremely difficult for even professors of the
English language to write it correctly. Possibly

there are, even in these criticisms, some errors
of my own; if so, they, too, will serve to teach
the same lesson, and make this fact more impressive, namely,—that to exercise the utmost
care and vigilance in composition is imperative on
every person who would acquire the honorable
distinction of being a graceful and powerful writer.

CRITICISM XVII.

EDWARD S. GOULD.

ONE of your correspondents, "H. S. D.", asks how I justify my use of the expression,—"I differ *with* Mr. Gould."

> "Custom", he says, "seems to have established the
> "use of *with* in such connection, *e. g.*, a member
> "of Parliament says without hesitation, 'I differ
> "*with* the honourable gentleman on that point
> "as widely as the east differs *from* the west.'
> "So, commonly, where opinions are concerned it
> "is 'differ *with*', in all other cases it is 'differ
> "'*from*'. It would interest some of us to hear
> "from Mr. Moon on this matter, if he thinks the
> "point worthy a moment's attention. How will
> "he justify our employing *with* to denote the
> "relation of separation, when its proper use
> "seems to be to express that of nearness, con-
> "tiguity?"

Before replying to this inquiry, I would say that the member of Parliament is blamable for "darkening counsel by words without know-

" ledge ", in attempting to illustrate a difference of opinion by instituting a comparison between it and something to which it cannot possibly bear any resemblance—the difference between east and west.

The objects to be gained by the use of comparisons are various : the elucidation of that which is obscure, the enhancement of that which we wish to exalt, and the depreciation of that which we wish to abase. The full power of this form of speech is seen when moral qualities are compared with moral, and physical with physical. But, in the instance under consideration, the honourable member differed with his friend in *opinion*; whereas, the east does not differ from the west in *opinion*. Hence, the incongruity. We might as well say of a man's sympathies, that they are as broad as the Mississippi : or of a woman's affections, that they are as deep as the Atlantic, as speak of a difference of opinion as being comparable to the difference between certain points of the compass. The fault of such expressions consists in this :—"*width*", "*breadth*", and " *depth*", of opinions, sympathies, and affections, are spoken of as if they were things palpable,—which could be defined, if not actually

measured; they are, however, but metaphorical
expressions relating to qualities existing merely
in the imagination.

Now let us consider the question of " differ
with" and "differ *from*". " H. S. D." says
that ;—" Commonly, where opinions are con-
" cerned, it is ' differ *with*'; in all other cases it
" is ' differ *from*'". These words imply that the
use of the preposition "*with*" is rendered necessary whenever it is opinions, and not things,
which form the topic of conversation. But, that
this is not the reason why that preposition is
used "*in such connection*" will be apparent when
we consider, that although we say ;—"I differ
"*with* you in opinion", we never say ;—"My
" opinion differs *with* yours", but always,—"My
" opinion differs *from* yours". As, then, it is
not the circumstance that the conversation is
concerning *opinions*, that makes us use the preposition "*with*"; is it that the pronoun is in
the nominative case, seeing that we say ;—"*I*
"differ *with* you in opinion", but,—"*My* opinion
" differs *from* yours "? No; that cannot be the
reason; for we say, not only ;—*I* differ *with*
" you in opinion "; but also,—"*I* differ *from*
" you in stature". Wherein, then, is the reason

to be found?   It is, I think, in the varied meaning of the word *"differ"*.   That word has not
the same meaning in the expression,—I *differ*
with you in opinion", as it has in the expression, —"I *differ from* you in stature."   In the
former, it has an active, in the latter, a passive,
signification.   In the one, the thing to be expressed is an act of the will; and " I differ *with*
"you on that point", is equivalent to,—" I
" wrestle with you", " I contend with you", " I
" dispute with you on that point, and you with
" me ".   The dispute is mutual.   But in the
expression, "I differ *from* you in stature", the
will is passive; the statement is concerning a
fact about which there cannot be any dispute, as
it means merely,—" In stature I am different
" from you."

   So, likewise, is it with the opposite of the word
" *differ*", the word " *agree*", *e. g.;*—I agree
" *with* you".   It is a mutual agreement; hence,
the propriety of saying, "*with* you".   But we do.
not say;—" I agree *with* your proposition"; we
say;—" I agree *to* your proposition"; there is
nothing mutual between me and the proposition,
therefore, I cannot say;—" I agree *with* it"; but
must say;—" I *agree to* it", *i. e.,* "I *assent to* it."

We cannot always trace the gradual process of unconscious reasoning which has been going on, in the mind of a people, in the formation of the idioms of their language; but it is always an interesting study. For example, we say;—"A "man parts *with* his wife"; we likewise say;— "A man parts *from* his wife." A man parts *with* his wife lovingly, regretfully, and looks hopefully forward to a reunion. A man parts *from* his wife angrily, and rushes off in a rage to the divorce court to obtain a judicial separation; and afterwards, whether the separation is confirmed by law or not, we still speak of the husband and wife as having parted *from* each other. The feud between them resulting in such an act is considered to be so bitter that, although the parting is mutual, the language which we employ respecting it, represents them not as *agreeing* to part, but represents each as acting *independently of the other*.

"H. S. D." is wrong in saying that in such expressions as, "I differ *with* the honourable "gentleman", we employ *with* "to denote the "relation of separation". We employ it to denote the relation of union. It may be a union of antagonistic qualities, a meeting for combat;

but still it is a union, a meeting for some purpose or other. " H. S. D." will probably acqui-
esce in my opinion respecting the word "*agree*",
as given above. But the same remarks that are
applicable to that word, are applicable to its
opposite, "*disagree*". I *agree with* one man, and
I *disagree with* another; "*with*" in each case
implies *union*. In the one, it is a union of
friendship, an embrace; in the other, a union of
antagonism, a death-grapple.

By a figure of speech, we attribute life and
volition to inanimate and to unconscious objects;
and we say;—"His food *disagrees with* him"; but
it is because we figuratively attribute life and
volition to the food and to the stomach, and
think of them as quarrelling, that we use the
preposition "*with*" in that sentence. If "H. S. D."
objects to the expression " *differ with*", he must,
in order to be consistent, object also to the expression "*disagree with*". But it would be perfectly good English, though perhaps not exactly
in good taste, to say ;—"A certain cannibal *dis-*
"*agreed with* one of his wives, killed her, and ate
" her; his troubles, however, did not end then,
" for she *disagreed with* him after he had eaten
" her, and he sickened and died."

I have now to notice Mr. Gould's reply to my criticisms on his ' *Good English* '. He acknowledges himself wrong on some points, differs with me in opinion upon others, and apologizes generally for the errors in his book by saying that he " *sometimes read the proof-sheets super-* " *ficially.*" Mr. Gould has much to learn in the school of letters if he thinks that the public will be satisfied with this explanation. Carelessness admits of no excuse. What is worth doing at all, is worth doing well; and, if we are justified in looking for perfection in language in any book, it certainly is in one which has been written to expose the errors of other writers. Besides, Mr. Gould should bear in mind what he says on that point respecting Archbishop Trench and Dean Alford. *See* page 121.

Mr. Gould pleads also that it is a first edition, which I have reviewed, and that

> "A first edition is never free from typographical and "other blunders."

Probably not; but the purchasers of a first edition have a right to the best that the author could produce at the time, and they are naturally indignant when, having unwittingly purchased

a book abounding with errors, they are coolly
told by the author, that he "*sometimes read the
"proof-sheets superficially.*"   As to the statement
that the errors will be corrected in the second
edition, what satisfaction is that to those persons
who have purchased the first?

Moreover, Mr. Gould's plea, respecting "a first
"edition", sounds very strange to those who
remember that he says, in his preface;—

> "*Many* of the following hints on philology *have*
> "*already appeared in print* in the form of occa-
> "sional contributions, through a series of years,
> "to newspapers and periodical publications; [w̲h̲y̲
> "'*and* periodical publications'?   Is not a '*news-*
> "'*paper*' a periodical publication?]—chiefly in
> "'*The New York Evening Post*'."

The strictures on '*Webster's Orthography*' likewise, which form the second part of the work,
are a reprint, with modifications, from '*The
'Democratic Review*', whence, we are told, they
were copied into several of the daily and weekly
papers of New York, Boston, and Philadelphia.
The last part, a treatise on *Clerical Elocution,*
is likewise a reprint: it appeared in '*The Boston
'Church Monthly*' and in '*The New York Chris-
'tian News*'.

Mr. Gould's plea, therefore, that the errors are those of a "*first edition*", is not likely to have much weight in influencing any one's judgment in his favour. On the contrary, this defence is weak and impolitic. In it he endeavours to intrench himself in a position which is untenable; and thereby he courts attack under disadvantageous circumstances, and exposes himself to censure for bad generalship.

CRITICISM XVIII.

EDWARD S. GOULD.

In my last criticism I commented upon the apologies which Mr. Gould had put forth for certain acknowledged errors in his '*Good English*'; which apologies are, that the work is in the first edition, and that he sometimes read the proof-sheets superficially. I have now to revert to certain disputed errors which he defends, and to notice the defence itself; and I do this the less reluctantly because one error speciously defended is productive of more evil than would result from a dozen errors which might justly be attributed to inadvertence.

I regret that anything in my criticisms should · have given offence to Mr. Gould. I regret that he should have taken offence when no offence was intended. He who assumes the office of public critic, should himself be prepared to submit to the ordeal of public criticism through

which he makes others pass. Mr. Gould, while
praising in general terms the accuracy of my
language in ' *The Dean's English* ', commented
upon what he considered to be errors of mine
in that book. For his correction, or for any
other person's correction, of any real errors of
mine, I am, and always shall be, sincerely
thankful. I no more lay claim to infallibility
than I do to omniscience. I endeavour to impart
to others whatever knowledge I have acquired;
and I am always glad to receive instruction in
return. The reviewers will find that I freely
avail myself of their criticisms, in order to make
each successive edition which I issue, more
worthy of public esteem than was the previous
one.

In criticising Mr. Gould's work, then, I have
but followed the example which he set me—he
first criticised mine—and I am not conscious of
having in any way spoken discourteously of him.
His book might be made a valuable contribution
to English philology, and one that would be read
with advantage by all. But it is not perfect yet;
and his defence of the errors which have been
pointed out in it is, both in matter and in manner,
anything but praiseworthy. Concerning my

criticisms on his '*Good English*', and his replies
to those criticisms, he says ;—

> " My modest [!] belief is, that he [Mr. Moon] will
> " learn from my criticisms on his essays, more
> " than I have learned from his criticisms on my
> " book."

It would be unbecoming in me to contend with
Mr. Gould on this delicate point. Indeed, it is
quite unnecessary for me to do so. I admit that
I *have* learnt from his criticisms more than it is
probable that he has learnt from mine. Let me
enumerate my gains from this source :—I have
learnt from Mr. Gould's example, that a writer
on the proprieties of language may say, of a
certain Latin quotation respecting matters of
taste, that ;—

> " The proverb ıs *something musty* " *!*

An expression quoted, indeed, from Shakspeare,
but one that is not the less inelegant on that
account.

I have learnt also that it is not considered
inelegant to say of a certain word ;—

> " It *smacks* of attempted prettiness in style ";

and that we may even intensify the expression
and say ;—

" ' I-ther' and 'ni-ther' *smack strongly* " of peculiarity, etc.

I have learnt likewise that a corrector of the
English of other writers may, himself, indulge in
slang, and say ;—

> " If he attempts [this should be *attempt*] to imitate
> " the style of another, however good that style
> " may be in the original, he will certainly *come to*
> " *grief* " !

Moreover, I have learnt that there are very
valuable privileges attaching to the office of public
critic ; privileges, from the enjoyment of which, unfortunately, my ignorance of their existence had
previously debarred me.   Thanks to Mr. Gould,
I now see that it is quite admissible for a critic to
palliate, in his own writings, the errors which he
censures in the writings of an other.   Mr. Gould's
illustrations of this are most simple and appropriate.   The following is his condemnation of
Dean Alford's misplacing of the adverb *" only "*.
I quote from ' *Good English* ', pp. 132, 133 :—

> " *Queen's English* ', paragraph 9.—" It is said also
> " *only to occur* three times ", etc.   Read, " occur
> " *only three times* ".
> Par. 44.—" this doubling *only takes place* in a syllable ",
> etc.   Read, " takes place *only in a syllable* ".

Par. 142.—"which can *only be decided* when those
"circumstances are known". Read, "can be
"decided *only when*", etc.

„ 166.—"I will *only say* that it produces", etc.
Read, "I will say *only that it produces*".

„ 170.—"It is said that this can *only be filled in*
"thus". Read, "can be filled in *only thus*".

„ 210.—"It can *only be used* as expressing determi-
"nation". Read, "can be used *only as expressing*
"*determination*".

„ 221.—"This . . . *only conveys* the sense", etc.
Read, "conveys *only the sense*".

„ 233.—"I can *only regard* them as Scotticisms".
Read, "regard them *only as Scotticisms*".

„ 289.—"and also when it is *only true* of them
"taken together". Read, "true of them *only*
"*when taken together*".

„ 368.—"I can *only deal* with the complaint in a
"general way". Read, "deal with the complaint
"*only in a general way*".

So also, on page 60 of '*Good English*', as
previously remarked, Mr. Gould condemns the
same error in a work by Archbishop Trench, from
which he quotes as follows :—"It is undoubtedly
"becoming different from what it has been, but
"*only different* in that it is passing into another
"stage of its development". Mr. Gould adds,
"this should be, '*different only*'." But when a

M

similar error is pointed out in Mr. Gould's '*Good*
'*English*', (see *Criticism* xv,) Oh! that is quite
an other thing.   It is clearly right to condemn
the expression "*only different*", in a sentence of
Archbishop Trench's; but it is not at all right to
condemn the expression "*only takes*", in a sentence of Mr. Gould's.   The simple reason for
which is, that *it is Mr. Gould's :*—an admirable
illustration of the old saying,—"Orthodoxy means
"*my doxy,* heterodoxy means *an other man's doxy.*"

It really is very delightful to be a critic, and
to be thus privileged in one's use of expressions ;
and I am deeply indebted to Mr. Gould for
opening my eyes to the riches of my inheritance ;
and, in his compassion for my ignorance, kindly
multiplying examples of the way in which my
wealth may be advantageously employed.   If I
condemn an author for writing so ambiguously
"as to leave the reader in doubt whether certain
"words relate to what immediately precedes, or
"to what follows them", (see '*Good English*', p.
110,) and am afterward caught in the commission
of the same error, (see *Criticism* xvi,) and the
public are challenged to come to any definite
conclusion as to which of two meanings I intended to convey, I perceive that the proper

course to adopt is, to act on the old showman's
principle, and tell my critics to " *take their*
" *choice* ".

This is indeed politic; and, in these days of
plagiarism, when distinctions between *meum* and
tuum are often utterly ignored, we cannot value
too highly the example which Mr. Gould sets us,
in drawing, as he does, a very broad line between
what is his own, and what is an other's.   For
example, in ' *The Queen's English* ', the Dean of
Canterbury uses the expression, "*more decisive*";
Mr. Gould objects to it, and asks;—" Does the
" Dean hold that ' *decisive* ' is an adjective that
" admits of comparison ? "   But when a similar
question is put to Mr. Gould respecting his use
of the expressions, " *so universally* " and " *so*
"*totally* ", and he is reminded that a *decision*, in
a court of law, for instance, may be confirmed
by a higher tribunal, and thereby be made "*more*
"*decisive*"; but that "*universality*" and "*to-*
"*tality*" cannot possibly be otherwise than
perfect or complete; he very wisely abstains from
entering upon any defence of the condemned
expressions, and says, with amusing brevity,
that he does not assent to his critic's objection.

In a former criticism I stated that Mr. Gould

speaks of a word under the similitude of a
counterfeit coin, and afterward of its being
"*purified*" by an "*endorsement*". Mr. Gould,
in refutation of the charge, says ;—

> " I beg leave to assure Mr. Moon that I do *not* speak
> " of a word '*as a coin* '. The word '*coin*' is not
> " in that part of my book. I speak of the making,
> " passing, and circulating of *currency* (which, if
> " I must again for Mr. Moon's benefit refer to a
> " dictionary, means '*paper passing for money* ')."

Mr. Gould seems to be determined to lay me
under obligation to him. He not only searches
out the word " *currency* " for me, in " *a diction-*
"*ary,* (it is to be regretted that he did not give
the title of the dictionary,) but he very consider-
ately selects for me the one special meaning
which *he* considers applicable. This is the more
kind, inasmuch as I have been unable to find
that particular, exclusive meaning in any of our
principal modern dictionaries. I have searched
Worcester, Webster, Richardson, Ogilvie, Craig,
and Chambers, but all in vain. I judge, therefore, that so far from its being *the* meaning of
" *currency* ", it is only a secondary meaning of
the word ; probably an Americanism. From
Johnson and Walker, it is true, I learn that the

word "*currency*" was formerly used for *paper* "*passing for money in the colonies*". But unless Mr. Gould is prepared to show that this is its *exclusive* meaning; *i.e.*, that it does *not* mean *coin* likewise, he cannot justly censure me for saying that he spoke of *coin* when he used the word *currency*. "*Currency*" is a term which is applicable to anything which passes *current* as money. "Abraham weighed to Ephron four hundred "shekels of silver, *current* money with the "merchant": Gen. xxiii, 16. When, therefore, I stated that Mr. Gould speaks of a word under the similitude of a *coin*, while, as he says, he really speaks of a word under the similitude of "*paper passing for money*", the cause of the error must, in justice, be attributed to him for his having used, in a conventional and restricted sense, the word "*currency*", which is a general term for "the *aggregate* of coin, notes, bills, etc., "in circulation in a country". If I have been misled as to Mr. Gould's meaning, it is his language which has misled me; for he not only speaks of *spurious currency*, but of its being unconsciously accepted as genuine, and mixed up and paid out with "*standard currency*". Surely this language is more applicable to *coin*, than to

paper, seeing that, according to the '*Encyclopædia
'Britannica*', 8th edition, Vol xv, p. 430, "by the
"*standard* of money is meant the degree of
"purity or fineness of the *metal* of which *coins*
"are made, and the quantity or weight of such
"metal in them". But Mr. Gould's use of the word
"*currency*" is objectionable for an other reason:
he uses the word as if it were synonymous with
promissory note; whereas, the word is descriptive not of *a part*, merely, but of *the whole*—"*the
"aggregate* of coin, notes, bills, etc., in circula-
"tion in a country". A promissory note may be
current, as legal tender; but it is not "*currency*";
and the calling it that, is a technical use of the
word which a writer on the proprieties of language
ought not to adopt. But granting, for the sake of
argument, that "*currency*" means *a promissory
note*, I have still to learn how a promissory note
can be *purified* by an *endorsement*.

CRITICISM XIX.

EDWARD S. GOULD.

THE principal charge which Mr. Gould brings against ' *The Dean's English* ' is, that in certain passages in it there are nouns which are followed by present participles, and yet are not in the possessive case. For instance, I say, on page 42 ;—" I spoke of *editors* falling into mistakes ". Again, page 56 ;—" We may properly speak of a "*word* being not strictly a neuter substantive, "but we cannot properly speak of a *substantive* " being strict ". Mr. Gould says ;—

> " The three italicized words should be in the posses-
> " sive case."

I have well weighed Mr. Gould's opinion upon this matter; I have consulted the highest authorities upon it, and I am compelled still to differ with Mr. Gould. There *are* passages in ' *The Dean's* ' *English* ' which I had considered would be better with the noun in the possessive case; and, in the present English edition of the work, they stand so; but in none of the instances quoted should Mr. Gould's alteration be made; as I will prove to him by quotations from an authority *to which he himself has appealed.*

I did not intend to reply to Mr. Gould's comments on this subject, because, fully to discuss it would occupy more space than could be devoted to it here. It fills fourteen closely printed large octavo pages in G. Brown's *' Grammar of English ' Grammars'.* Still, lest, being silent, my silence should be misconstrued, and a wrong impression be produced as to the value which I set upon Mr. Gould's remarks concerning nouns which precede present participles, I will quote a few passages from the valuable work just mentioned (second edition); merely prefacing those passages by the statement that I entirely agree with the opinions which they express :—

Page 503.—"Though the *ordinary* syntax of " the possessive case is sufficiently plain and " easy, there is, perhaps, among all the puzzling " and disputable points of grammar, nothing " more difficult of decision than are some " questions that occur respecting the right " management of this case."

Page 642.—"The observations which have

" been made . . . show that possessives before
" participles are *seldom* to be approved."

Page 642.—" This brings us again to that
" difficult and apparently unresolvable problem,
" whether participles as such, by virtue of their
" mixed gerundive character, can, or cannot,
" govern the possessive case ; a question, about
" which, the more a man examines it, the more
" he may doubt."

Page 643.—" The following example, from
" ' *West's Letters* ', is manifestly inconsistent with
" itself; and, in my opinion, the three posses-
" sives are all wrong : ' The kitchen too now
" ' begins to give dreadful note of preparation ;
" ' not from *armorers* accomplishing the knights,
" ' but from the *shopmaid's* chopping force-meat,
" ' the *apprentice's* cleaning knives, and the
" ' *journeyman's* receiving a practical lesson in
" ' the art of waiting at table.' It should be :
" ' not from *armorers* accomplishing the knights,
" ' but from the *shopmaid* chopping force-meat,
" ' the *apprentice* cleaning knives, and the *jour-
" ' neyman* receiving,' etc. The nouns are the
" principal words, and the participles are ad-
" juncts."

Page 643.—" The leading word in sense ought

"not to be made the adjunct in the construction;
"and the participle, if it remain such, ought
"rather to relate to its noun, as being the
"adjunct, than to govern it in the possessive
"case, as being the principal term."

Page 643.—"'The daily instances of *men's*
"'dying around us.' Say rather, 'of *men* dying
"'around us'."

Page 644.—"If such relations between the
"participle and the objective be disapproved,
"*the substitution of the possessive case is liable to*
"*still stronger objections.*"

There is nothing concerning which Mr. Gould
manifests more ignorance, than concerning the
rules which govern the possessive case of nouns;
and, as might have been expected, there is nothing
concerning which he speaks more dogmatically.
It does not seem to have occurred to him, that
upon puzzling questions, which scholars have
been unable satisfactorily to settle, it behoves
us to speak with diffidence.

Concerning "that difficult and apparently un-
"resolvable problem, whether participles as
"such, by virtue of their mixed gerundive
"character, can, or cannot, govern the possessive case", Goold Brown, we see, says;—

it is " a question, about which, the more a man " examines it, the more he may doubt." As this is the opinion of one who is well qualified to judge of the matter, we can have no hesitation in determining why it is that Mr. Gould has not any doubts respecting it.

In replying to an inquiry put by H. S. D., I said ;—" We might as well speak of the breadth " of a man's sympathies' being as great as the " breadth of the Mississippi ; or of the depth of a " woman's affections' being as great as the depth " of the Atlantic ; as speak of a difference of " opinions' being comparable to the difference " between certain points of the compass." I believe that, in the manuscript which I sent from London, the three words, *sympathies, affections,* and *opinions*, in the foregoing sentence, were each in the possessive case ; but, by an error of the printer in New York, the sign of the possessive case was omitted from the last of them ; and as I have no chance of even *"superficially"* reading the proof sheets of my criticisms in ' *The Round Table* ', I am naturally exposed to censure for what is really not my fault : and several weeks must unavoidably elapse before I have an opportunity of freeing myself, as in this case, from a charge of inconsistency. However, I must say that I am not in very great fear that my character for accuracy and consistency will suffer much from that cause; for, as respects my own criticisms generally, I can testify that they are printed in ' *The Round Table* ' with extraordinary fidelity to the original.

Had I to rewrite the sentence which is at present under consideration, I should slightly alter the wording of it; (it is altered in this edition;) for I agree with the author of ' *The Grammar of English Grammars* ', that it is generally better to avoid using possessives before present participles. Still, I am glad that I did not avoid that construction in the instance to which I refer, as it has been the means of drawing forth Mr. Gould's opinion upon a subject which is deserving of notice.

He says, in speaking of his own criticisms on the possessive case ;—

> " But while Mr. Moon tacitly admits the propriety of
> " my criticism, and evinces a disposition to follow
> " *it,* he shows that after all, he does not under-
> " stand *it.* He, indeed, uses the possessive
> " [sign] in sentences which require *it;* [why
> " make three consecutive clauses end with the

"same little pronoun *it ?*] but he applies it to the
"*wrong nouns.*" Mr. Gould goes on to say;—"The
"reader, by referring to Mr. Moon's fourth
"essay, will see that Mr. Moon speaks of the use
"and abuse of *comparisons;* and that, to illus-
"trate his point, he selects the words *breadth,*
"*depth,* and *difference.* Those words are his
"terms of comparison, and therefore those words,
"and not *sympathies, affections,* and *opinions,*
"should be in the possessive case. Mr. Moon
"will no doubt deny that; but, observe, in the
"sentence above quoted, Mr. Moon does not
"bring ' sympathies' and ' Mississippi' nor ' affec-
"' tions ' and ' Atlantic ' into comparative oppo-
"sition; his words are 'the *breadth* of a man's
"' sympathies ' being as great as the *breadth* of
"' the Mississippi; or the *depth* of a woman's
"'affections ' being as great as the *depth* of the
"' Atlantic ', etc."

Let us examine this statement. Mr. Gould
says that, in the sentence which he has quoted,
I have *applied the possessive* to the wrong nouns.
He means that I have applied *the sign* of the
possessive case to the wrong nouns. He says
that *"breadth", "depth",* and *"difference"* are
my terms of comparison, *"and therefore those*
"words, and not 'sympathies', 'affections', and
"' opinions', should be in the possessive case."
This reasoning is plausible, but its fallacy will

be evident when I point out that my terms of comparison are *not* "breadth", "depth", and "difference'. These are abstract terms; and my terms are not *abstract,* but *specific.* I do not speak of comparing "*breadth*", in the abstract, with "*the breadth of the Mississippi;* but "*the "breadth of a man's sympathies*", with "*the "breadth of the Mississippi*". Nor do I speak of comparing "*depth*", in the abstract, with "*the "depth of the Atlantic*"; but "*the depth of a "woman's affections*", with "*the depth of the "Atlantic*"; and if Mr. Gould does not know, he *ought* to know before presuming to write upon the subject, that—"the possessive sign is "sometimes annexed to that part of a compound "name, which is, of itself, in the objective case; "as 'The *Lord Mayor of London's* authority'." If we were to apply Mr. Gould's reasoning to this expression, we should have to say that, as it is not *London's* authority, but *the Lord Mayor's* authority that is meant, *London ought not to be in the possessive case!* But, of a similar sentence, '*The Grammar of English Grammars*' says, on page 511, that the two nouns "cannot be ex- "plained separately as forming two cases, but "must be parsed together as *one name* governed "in the usual way". So, in my sentence, the nominatives to the participle "*being*", are not, as Mr. Gould affirms, "*breadth*" and "*depth*"; but are "*the-breadth-of-a-man's-sympathies*" and "*the-depth-of-a-woman's-affections*"; and "*any phrase* "or *sentence* which is made the subject of a finite "verb, must be taken in the sense of *one thing*, "and be spoken of as *a whole*":—'*Grammar of* '*English Grammars*', page 573; and, of course, the sign of the possessive case must be, at the end, as Lindley Murray says;—"a phrase in "which the words are so connected and depen- "dent, as to admit of no pause before the con- "clusion, necessarily requires the genitive sign "at or near *the end* of the phrase".—'*English Grammar*', 8vo. edition, Vol. 1, page 263.

Let it be noticed that the matter in dispute here, between Mr. Gould and me, is not the apparently unresolvable problem as to whether participles, as such, can or cannot govern the possessive case. Mr. Gould requires the nouns preceding present participles *to be* in the pos- sessive case; and in my sentence they *are* so. Nor is it a question between us, which word should have been in the possessive case, *had my sentence been differently constructed;* for, Mr. Gould,

himself, says of that very sentence ;—"*the gram-*
"*matical construction of a sentence depends on the*
"*words that a man uses, and not on those that*
"*he might have used.*"   Mr. Gould's remarks,
therefore, apply to my sentence, *as it stands;*
and of *it* he says, that the sign of the possessive
case is therein applied "*to the wrong nouns*".

On the highest authority, then, namely that
of Goold Brown, and also on the authority of
Lindley Murray, I deny the justice of Mr. E. S.
Gould's strictures on my sentence; and I affirm
that the ignorance which they betray, of the
commonest rules governing the possessive case,
is such as would disgrace the merest tyro in
composition.

Mr. Gould has again adverted to my condemnation of his too frequent use of the little
word "*so*".   He is evidently not at ease respecting it; or he would, after what has been said
on the subject, have let the matter rest.   As,
however, he has not done so, but has resorted to
desperate means to improve his position, I cannot
but conclude that he considered it to be critical.

Now, of the many desperate means to which
men in critical positions resort, none is more
fraught with danger, than is dishonesty; and

though I should be sorry to make any condem-
natory charge reflecting on Mr. Gould's character
as a controvertist; still, I must say that his
conduct, in the matter under consideration, so
much *resembles* literary dishonesty, that I hope
he will, in justice to himself, give us a satisfactory explanation of the following singular
circumstances.

Respecting certain remarks of mine on the
word "*so*", he first makes a statement which is
not in accordance with the facts of the case,
and he endeavours to support that statement by
a fictitious quotation of words *nowhere to be found
in my criticism;* and then, feeling, I suppose,
that he has done a very foolish thing, he is
constrained to write again upon the subject, and
correct his quotation of the passage; but, as if
his evil genius *would not* forsake him, he is
tempted to omit from the middle of the dozen
lines which he quotes, the very words which are
opposed to his assertion, and which convict him
of having unjustly charged me with incorrectness!

In speaking of Mr. Gould's expressions, "*so*
"totally", and "*so* universally", I had said;—
"To use language implying that anything can be
"universal, and yet only partly universal; or

N

"total, and yet only partly total, is to speak
"nonsensically; yet such is the import of Mr.
"Gould's expressions, '*so* universally', '*so*
"totally'." I might have added that Mr.
Gould, not content with this murdering of the
Queen's English, "out-Herods Herod" and says,
'*Good English*', page 100 ;—

"*So absolutely universal*"!

Of all the outrageously extravagant examples
of this kind of error that I ever met with, none
equals this of Mr. Gould's. I wonder whether
he will object to my condemnation of it. He
said of my remarks on his similar expressions;—"Neither do I assent to his objection
"to *so universally* and *so totally*". As Mr. Gould
is frequently asking me for my authorities, I
will tell him what they say on this matter.
I have not always brought forward my authorities; because I gave Mr. Gould credit for
being sufficiently well read in grammar to render
that course unnecessary.

Dr. Crombie says ;—"*Universal* is an ad-
"jective, whose signification cannot be height-
"ened or lessened; it therefore rejects all
"intensive and diminutive words, as, *so, more,*

"less, least, most".—*Treatise on Etymology and Syntax*, page 359.

Lindley Murray says ;—"Adjectives that have "in themselves a superlative signification, do "not properly admit of the superlative or com- "parative form superadded. The phrases, so "perfect, so right, so extreme, *so universal*, etc., "are incorrect".—'*English Grammar*', 8vo. edition, Vol. 1, page 250.

Goold Brown says ;—"Comparative termi- "nations, and adverbs of degree, should not be "applied to adjectives that are not susceptible "of comparison ; as, '*So universal* a complaint'." —'*Grammar of English Grammars*', page 543.

After condemning Mr. Gould's expressions, "*so* "*universally*", and "*so totally*", I said ;—"The "little word '*so*' is often misused in Mr. Gould's "'*Good English*'. It occurs four times in four "consecutive lines on page 213". I then quoted the passage, and added, "*This is the very opposite* "*of elegant*". It must, therefore have been obvious to every reader, except "*superficial*" Mr. Gould, that my condemnation of the passage was for its want of *elegance*—its tautology. In- deed, there is strong presumptive evidence that this was obvious to him also, or he would not, in

endeavouring to support his previous statement,
have omitted, from his quotation of my remark,
the words,—"*this is the very opposite of elegant*";
and have charged me with having said that he
had "four times misused the word *so*",—misused it by using it *in a sense not consistent with
its meaning;* see '*Round Table*', vol. 6, page 89.
My words are not,—*the misuse* occurs four times
in four consecutive lines;—but, "*it* [the little
"word *so*] occurs four times in four consecutive
"lines......*This is the very opposite of elegant*".
Had I said, "*the misuse* of the little word '*so*'
"is frequent in Mr. Gould's '*Good English*'";
then the "*it*", might have applied to "*the mis-
"use*"; but the words are not,—"*the misuse is
"frequent*"; the words are,—"*the little word 'so'*
"*is frequently misused*"; the "*it*", therefore,
must apply to the word "*so*".

Mr. Gould's charge, then, falls to the ground;
or rather, it stands as an additional evidence of
his superficial reading; for I attribute to that,
and not to any intentional dishonesty on his
part, his strange omission of the most important
words in that portion of the paragraph which he
pretended to quote from my criticism. I advise
him, as he values his literary reputation, to be

more careful in future. The superficial reading of an opponent's remarks may be passed over; even a false statement which is based upon that superficial reading may be pardoned; but a subsequent deliberate supporting of that false statement, by a garbled quotation of an opponent's words, is a course of action which is very likely to result in dishonour.

CRITICISM XX.

EDWARD S. GOULD.

To please Mr. Gould, who seems to be very
anxious to prolong this controversy, I continue
my criticisms on his language. I am delighted
to serve him; he is not a hard task-master,—
one requiring me to "*make bricks without straw*".
He gives me plenty of the latter material; and,
knowing that it has been only "*superficially*"
thrashed, expects · that I shall thrash it
thoroughly. His expectations shall not be dis-
appointed; nor shall any of his straw be wasted;
for, what is not used in making bricks for a
monument to be erected to his memory, shall be
conscientiously made into *chaff*. In justification
of my using such an expression as "*chaff*", I
refer the reader to page 160.

Mr. Gould flatters himself that the errors
which I have exposed are all which are to be
found in his work; and that I close my criticisms because I am, as he elegantly says,

"*hard pushed*"—"*short of materials to work upon*".

So far from that being the case, there are,

even now, in my note-book, more than forty
errors of his upon which I have not yet commented. I have left them unnoticed merely on
account of their being similar to those which I
have previously criticised. The fact that Mr.
Gould, in common with other writers, has committed those errors, does not seem to me to be
of sufficient importance to warrant my asking
for space in ' *The Round Table* ' to expose them.

Errors *abound* in Mr. Gould's work. I had not
intended to speak of any more, but his defiant
mode of meeting criticism prevents my dealing
with him as leniently as I otherwise would. I
will take five consecutive pages, 20, 21, 22, 23,
and 24 ; and, by exposing the errors in them,
will show how forbearingly I have hitherto criticised his work, in that I altogether passed over
those errors. On page 20, he says of the word
donate ;—

"Webster, of course, records the word; and he
"gravely gives its etymology 'from *donare,*
"'*donatum*', etc.,—as if the *prig* [!] who fabri-
"cated that *bit* [!] of literature ever saw a Latin
"dictionary, or ever heard of the Latin lan-
"guage!"

Are these suitable expressions to use when
condemning the inelegancies of other writers?

On page 21, I read ;—

"If Mr. Everett were about to deliver his oration on
"Washington, at the Academy of Music."

"*On Washington, at the Academy of Music*"!
Mr. Gould should have said ;—"deliver, at the
"Academy of Music, his oration on Washington".
Turn to the next page, 22 ; there we read ;—

"That is, the addition of *ess* to those nouns which
"indicate persons, in order to designate females".

"*Nouns which indicate persons, in order to
"designate females*"! Why did not Mr. Gould
arrange his words somewhat in this manner ?—
"That is, the designating of women, by the
"addition of *ess* to those nouns which indicate
"persons generally."
On page 23, we are told of certain words

"which have become as *plenty* as blackberries";

instead of "as *plentiful* as blackberries." Dr.
Campbell, in his '*Philosophy of Rhetoric*', says,
Vol. 1, page 417 ;—"*Plenty* for *plentiful* appears
"to me so gross a vulgarism that I should not
"have thought it worthy a place here, if I had
"not sometimes found it in works of considerable
"merit." Johnson says ;—"It is used *barbarously*

"for 'plentiful'." Shakspeare uses the expression, but it is generally condemned.

On page 24, Mr. Gould, in speaking of the word "*firstly* ", says ;—

"No lexicographer has yet ventured to accredit it."

If Mr. Gould will refer to that dictionary of which, at page 167, he speaks thus :—" It is " simply justice to say, that Worcester's is the " only American dictionary which deserves to be " regarded as a standard of English orthogra- " phy", he will find, not only that the word is accredited, but, that authorities are given for its use.

I do not object to the occasional use of "*first* ", as an adverb; but, in sentences where it would be followed by " *secondly* ", " *thirdly* ", etc., the adverbial form is, I think, preferable.

Of the phrase, " I differ *with* him in opinion ", Mr. Gould says ;—

"Mr. Moon devotes to 'H. S. D.' no less than a "column and a half; and, as might be expected, "[Mr. Gould should have said;—'as might *have* "' *been* expected'. That of which he wrote was "*past*] he leaves the point as he found it; namely "an indefensible blunder, against which the taste, "the ear, and the common sense of every edu- "cated man revolt, as a matter of course."

As a matter of course, Mr. Gould's acquaintance with educated men qualifies him thus to speak; and equally *" as a matter of course "*, Dr. Worcester cannot be considered an educated man, seeing that he says, in his *' Dictionary of ' the English Language'*, page xi;—" Differ *with* " a person in opinion; *from* a person or thing " in some quality."

The same excellent work condemns Mr. Gould's strictures on the word *" graduated "*, which, he says, on page 102,—

> "requires some part of the verb *to be* before it,......
> "we might as well say *' he born '* as say *' he*
> "*' graduated'*."

Was there ever such nonsense written by one professing to teach the proper use of the English language? Worcester says;—

> "GRADUATE, *v. n.* To take a degree; to become a
> "graduate; to receive a diploma.—'He *graduated*
> "*'at Oxford'*."

Thus I might proceed, and fill column after column of the *' The Round Table '* with exposures of Mr. Gould's errors. He says;—

> "The quotation *would* suffice *if* Mr. Moon's rule on
> "affirmative expressions *is* correct, but I deny
> "its correctness."

A writer on the proprieties of language should know that the *foregoing sentence* is not correct. He should have said, either,—"The quotations "*would* suffice *if* Mr. Moon's rule *were* correct"; or,—"The quotations *will* suffice *if* Mr. Moon's "rule *is* correct."

After finding such errors as these, we cannot wonder that Mr. Gould speaks of Dean Alford's "*generally accurate style*".—'*Good English*', page 115. "Birds of a feather", etc.

Mr. Gould says;—

> "I would like [he means 'I *should* like'] to ask
> "why Mr. Moon uses the adjective *strange* for
> "the adverb *strangely* in this sentence:—'Mr.
> "'Gould's plea respecting a first edition sounds
> "'very *strange* to those who remember ',' etc.

It is evident from this remark that Mr. Gould would have said;—"it sounds very *strangely* to "those who remember", etc. *Strange* inconsistency! See what he says respecting the phrase, "*the trees looked magnificently*".—'*Good* '*English*', page 49. "*Looked*" has here a strictly neuter meaning, and therefore should be followed by an adjective; the phrase being, virtually, this:—the trees *appeared, to the eye,* magnificent. Now, I (not "*would like*", but) *should like* to know why *" sounded, to the ear "*, must be followed by an *adverb*, while *" appeared, " to the eye "*, must be followed by an *adjective.* If this is a specimen of Mr. Gould's teaching, those who accept him as their guide must be strangely puzzled by the instruction which they receive.

Mr. Gould seems to conclude that every adverse opinion of his which I do not controvert is accepted by me as being correct. I beg that on that point he will no longer deceive himself and his readers; for, it does not follow that, because I do not reply to a certain counter-criticism, I therefore assent to it. Here is an example of what I mean :—Mr. Gould had said ;—' *Good* ' *English* ', page 204.

"This passage is more commonly read *wrong* ", etc.

I expressed surprise that he had not used, after the active verb *" read "*, the adverb *" wrongly "*. He replied, that *" wrong "* is both an *adverb* and an *adjective*; and, consequently, that his sentence is correct. I did not consider the matter worth any more words, and therefore left his remarks unanswered; but as he has written again to ' *The Round Table* ' and said ;—

"In due time I trust [he should have said, ' *I trust*
" '*that in due time* '] I shall hear Mr. Moon's re-
"joinder to my comments on that point".

I give him my rejoinder thus :—I am aware
that "*wrong*" is frequently used adverbially. I
am aware also that G. Brown, in his ' *Grammar*
' *of English Grammars* ', pages 667, 670, says;—
"Adverbs that end in *ly*, are in general preferable
"to those forms which, for want of this dis-
"tinction, may seem like adjectives misapplied."
"Examples :—' By the numbers being con-
" ' founded, and the possessives *wrong* applied,
" ' the passage is neither English nor grammar.'
" '*Buchanan's Syntax* ', page 123. Better thus:—
" '*wrongly* applied', see page 980. Again,—
" ' The letter G is *wrong* named *jee* '. ' *Creighton's*
" ' *Dictionary* ', page 8. Better thus :—'*wrongly*
" ' named ', see page 980 ". As this is the
opinion of one to whom, as to an authority,
Mr. Gould has referred me, and very properly
so, I trust that he will now be satisfied.

With similar short-sightedness Mr. Gould
says ;—

"I find, moreover, that Mr. Moon frequently uses *so*
"in the same manner that [this should be '*in*
" 'the same manner *in which* '; see *Grammar of*

"'*English Grammars*', page 303] he tells me
"that demonstrative young ladies use it. Here
"is a sentence that contains a pair of them."

What! a pair of "*demonstrative young ladies*"?
Certainly; there is no other plural noun, in Mr.
Gould's sentence, that can be referred to by
his plural pronoun "*them*".

Mr. Gould says;—

"I *was* [*am*, vide seq.] agreeably surprised to find
"that the microscopic investigation of Mr. Moon
"*has, thus far*, detected so few errors in '*Good*
"*English*'—I mean so few *real* errors"!

It is a pity to disturb Mr. Gould's complaisant
satisfaction in his own work; but I must remark
that in the foregoing sentence there is one of
the drollest errors which a writer could possibly
commit. Mr. Gould says, in effect, that he is
surprised to find that a microscopic investigation of *me* has, thus far, detected so few errors
in '*Good English*'! I really was not aware that
I had been made the subject of microscopic investigation; and, even if I had, I should still be
at a loss to comprehend how such an investigation of me, could result in a detection of Mr.
Gould's errors. Does he imagine that my
perusal of his book has resulted in its errors

being photographed on the retina of my eye,
and that they are discoverable by means of the
microscope? A *"microscopic investigation of
"Mr. Moon"!* What next? The foregoing
nonsense is not the result of a printer's error,
but is an example of what is one of Mr. Gould's
usual modes of expression. I recommend him
carefully to consider the difference that there is
between the two following phrases :—" *A portrait
" of Mr. Gould,* and *"a portrait of Mr. Gould's".*
The former expression means a portrait of my
worthy antagonist; the latter may mean a
portrait of an old woman; and were I, in
speaking of it, to follow Mr. Gould's example,
and, dropping the possessive *'s,* call the portrait
of the old woman ;—"*A portrait of Mr. Gould"*,
I fancy that he would instantly awake to a consciousness of the absurdity of his own form of
speech.

Yet, one word more. Mr. Gould, writing to
' *The Round Table'* respecting those errors in
his book which he purposes correcting in future
editions, says ;—

> " I send you a list of the corrections, which you may
> "publish *if you think the game is worth the*
> " *candle* ".

I must pause to express my admiration of the beauty, the appositeness, and the classic elegance of this expression; one suitable enough in colloquial French—*" Le jeu ne vaut pas la chandelle"*— but quite out of place in a philological discussion. Mr. Gould says, after enumerating his errors;—

> "The foregoing list includes all the errors that I am
> "thus far aware of. Many things have been
> "specified by my critics which I do not admit to
> "be errors; and many notices of my book have
> "been published which I have not seen".

Mr. Gould has, undoubtedly, seen the notices of his book which have been published in ' *The* ' *Round Table*'; for he quotes from them. How is it, then, that he altogether ignores the exposure of that which has been there described as the " *climax* " of his errors? Is it really to be left unaltered in future editions? Speaking of the omission of the final '*s* at the end of proper names in the possessive case, Mr. Gould says, ' *Good English*', page 79 ;—

> " Byron made short work of that, when he wrote,—
>
>> " ' And ere the faithless truce was broke
>> " ' Which freed her from the unchristian yoke,
>> " ' With him his gentle daughter came ;
>> " ' Nor there since Menelaus's dame
>> " ' Forsook,' etc.

" In that case ", says Mr. Gould, "the printer may do
" what he pleases with the final *s*,—use it or omit
" it ; but the reader will take care to pronounce
" it—if he knows how to read ".

" If he knows how to pronounce ", says the
learned critic in '*The Round Table*', "the reader
"will take care to read the line in *this* manner :—

"'Nor there since Men-e-la-us' dame'—"

" in which we look in vain for Mr. Gould's pos-
" sessive *s*'".

Happily, Mr. Gould's ignorance of Greek
pronunciation is counterbalanced by the beauti-
fully modest diffidence which he manifests in
delivering his valuable opinion upon it.

Respecting "*the list of corrections* ", from which
Mr. Gould has omitted the above-mentioned gem,
he says, with amusing conceit, in a subsequent
letter ;—

I regard my list of corrections, as a damaging reply
" *(in anticipation) to Mr. Moon's present essay.*"

Little does Mr. Gould seem to know, that
when a man thus speaks in his own praise, his
doing so is accepted by all, as indisputable evidence that he considers it *necessary !*

o

CRITICISM XXI.

EDWARD S. GOULD.

So *"tautology"* does not mean *a repetition of the same word?*   Certainly not!   Mr. Gould has affirmed it ; and how can we be in doubt concerning any matter upon which *he* has spoken authoritatively?   Do we not remember his learned disquisition on the proper pronunciation of the name of the Greek hero *Men-e-lá-us!* Have we forgotten—can we ever forget—can we ever cease to fear—the threatened outpouring of that merciless scorn which Mr. Gould gives us to understand shall descend on our heads if we dare to pronounce that name otherwise than *Men-e-laus?*   His acquaintance with Greek is profound and I tremble while I venture to speak to him concerning the derivation of the word *" tautology"*.

He accuses me of ignorance :—I hang down my head, and blush as I acknowledge the justice of the accusation.   He assumes the possession of superior learning :—I look up ; and, timidly approaching him, ask to be instructed. He says that

> *'Tautology*" means "*a repetition of the same meaning*
> "*in different words*"; and that "a repetition of
> "the same word or words is another matter.
> "That is *merely* 'repetition', and is not at all
> "tautology. And to call it '*tautology*', as Mr.
> "Moon does, is to betray ignorance of the mean-
> "ing of the word".

Had I not the most unbounded confidence in the *thoroughness* of Mr. Gould's learning, I should imagine that he had accepted, with unquestioning faith, the erroneous opinion of some lexicographer in whom he has implicit confidence, and had not taken the trouble to analyze the word for himself. But as I know that he never does anything "*superficially*", I at once banish the idea, and trust that, in compassion for my "*ignorance*", he will condescend to let me know by what ingenious process of reasoning he arrived at the conclusion that ταυτολογια does *not* mean "*the same words*". Richardson—but who is Richardson? Edward S. Gould is the great authority on matters relating to Greek— nevertheless, Richardson says ;—

> "TAUTOLOGY. Gr. ταυτολογια, *the same words, or words*
> "*of the same signification.* A repetition or re-

o 2

"peated use of the same word or words of the
"same or equivalent signification." See the quo-
"tation from Warburton;—'A repetition of this
"'kind, made in *different words,* is called a pleo-
"'nasme: but when in the *same words* (as it is in
"'the text in question, if there be any repetition
"'at all) it is then *a tautology.'"

See also what Goold Brown says:—

"The repetition of the word *degree,* in saying, 'The
"superlative degree increases or lessens the
"positive to the highest or lowest '*degree*', is a
"disagreeable *tautology*."—Grammar of English
Grammars, page 279.

Again:—

"To say, 'The *numbers* must agree in *number* with
"'substantives', is *tautological*".—Page 316.

Mr. Gould concludes by saying;—

"I hope that Mr. Moon will henceforth keep quiet
"on '*tautology*'."

I do not doubt that the readers of '*The
'Round Table*' will, equally with myself, believe
in the sincerity of this expression of hope from
Mr. Gould. It must have been prompted by
the most disinterested of motives. Possibly,
he feared that I should bring upon myself the
overwhelming derision of scholars. He has my
warmest acknowledgments; and, if I further

rashly expose my *"ignorance"*, I trust that, whatever opinion others may entertain of the act, *he* will believe that I am influenced only by a desire not to be outdone in disinterestedness, seeing that I am still willing to let my darkness be the foil that shall best set off the lustre of his thoughts.

I do not consider tautology,—and by *"tautology"* I mean a repetition of the same word or words,— to be always a blemish in composition; on the contrary, I consider it to be often a beauty and a power, and that it frequently gives eloquence to the utterance, and force to the reasoning. In the following passage from my work, *'The Dean's 'English'*, page 110, I have, myself, used the word *"language"* eleven times in one sentence; and yet I have not, I believe, used it once too often. The passage is on the neglect of the study of English, and is as follows:—

"What a disgrace to us as Englishmen is
"this!—that our noble language,—the language
"of our prayers to the Throne of Heaven; the
"language of the dearest and holiest relation-
"ships of life; the language of the maternal lips
"which have blessed us and are now silent in the
"grave; the language of our sorrows and our

"joys, our aspirations and our regrets; the
"language in which we breathe our consolations
"to the dying, and our farewells to those whom
"we love; the language in which are embalmed
"the stirring appeals of our patriots, and the
"thrilling battle-cries of our warriors; the
"language of our funeral dirges over those who
"have fallen in defence of our homes, our
"children, and our liberties; the language in
"which have been sung our pæans of triumph
"in hours of victories which have made England
"great among the nations; that this language,
"—the language of Shakspeare, of Milton, and
"of the Bible, should be utterly ignored as a
"study in our schools and our colleges! This
"is indeed a disgrace; a disgrace such as the
"Greeks and Romans never incurred; and one
"upon which men in future ages of the world will
"look back with wonder."

Mr. Gould tells us that he is availing himself
of the advice of his friends. I hope that none
of them will be so indiscreet as to advise him to
discontinue his letters to ' *The Round Table* '.
They will certainly establish for him a reputation
which will last as long as the English language
is spoken.   Go on, Mr. Gould, in the path which

you have chosen; rewards, far greater than any
which you have yet received, await you in the
future.   But as there may be a wearying delay
before we shall be able to congratulate you on
the possession of those honours which you covet,
you will not, I am sure, object to our whiling
away a portion of the time by indulging in a
little innocent mirth at your expense.

> "Care to our coffin adds a nail, no doubt;
> *While every burst of laughter draws one out."

A man who begins to build, and is not able to
finish, has always been regarded as a proper
object at which to point the finger of ridicule.
Mr. Gould began to build a formidable battery,
on which he purposed to mount one of the
heaviest of his little guns, and then tempt me to
storm the position, that he might—do, I know
not what!

He said, as I have previously remarked;—

> "*I would like* to ask why Mr. Moon uses the adjective
> "*strange* for the adverb *strangely*, in this
> "sentence:—'*Mr. Gould's plea respecting a "first
> "*"*edition*" *sounds very strange to those who
> "'*remember*,' etc.   As Mr. Moon informs me
> "that 'carelessness admits of no excuse', I trust
> "that he will not *plead* 'carelessness' in answer-
> "ing this second enquiry."

Mr. Gould meant to say; — "will not, in "answering this second enquiry, plead 'care- "'lessness'." *Now*, however, Mr. Gould feels obliged to acknowledge that *my sentence* is perfectly correct, and that *his* "*question*" (as he foolishly calls it, for it is merely the expression of a desire, and contains nothing interrogatory,) was a blunder, "*a careless blunder*".

I do not like to contradict any man; but I must protest against Mr. Gould's calling this "a "*careless* blunder". There was no carelessness in it; it was a direct, *deliberate* charge of error preferred against me; and was, moreover, accompanied by an expression of trust that *I* should not plead carelessness as an excuse, in my answering the charge. He *believed* that in my sentence, which he quoted, the adverb "*strangely*" ought to have been employed, and not the adjective "*strange*"; this, even a child may see.

Mr. Gould rather astonished me by saying, when he accounted for the errors found in his '*Good English*', that he had "*read the proof- "sheets superficially*". But for his own assertion, I should never have believed that he, as an author writing to expose the errors of others, had acted in so silly a manner. However, I gave him credit for the carelessness behind which he sought shelter. Again, when he thought that it would answer his purpose to condemn ' *The* ' *Dean's English* ', upon which he had previously lavished his praise, and he felt that some apology would be expected for a change in his views which he foresaw would be regarded with suspicion, *superficial reading* was again the plea which he put forth. This, too, astonished me; but, once more I gave him credit for the carelessness behind which he sought shelter.

There is, however, a limit to every man's credulity, and now that Mr. Gould pleads *carelessness* a third time, and as an excuse for a very different kind of error, I feel bound to tell him that I think he has used a wrong word. A man may plead carelessness as a reader, and carelessness as a writer, and, consequently, be utterly unworthy of confidence as a professor of literature; but when he pleads *carelessness* as an excuse, not for the form of his sentences, but, for his deliberate statements themselves, he employs a term, of which the most polite thing that can be said, even in parliamentary language, is, that it is not justified by the facts of the case.

Like one groping his way in the dark, and

feeling about for something by which he may guide his steps, Mr. Gould repeatedly asks for authorities. But, surely, that which exists as a rule in grammar *merely* in virtue of its having been laid down by some once-celebrated gramma-rian, is valueless. Far better than all *such* authorities are the dictates of common sense, and a knowledge of the usages of the best society. I condemned Mr. Gould's use of *"would"* for *"should"* in the sentence, *"I would like"*. He attempts a defence of his expression, by say-ing ;—

> "I mean that, as a matter of choice, option, will, I
> *"would* like, and therefore my *'would'* is pure
> "English, Mr. Moon to the contrary, notwith-
> "standing".

"Mr. Gould then says, that if *"I would"* is incorrect, he really does not see "how Mr. Moon "can escape the consequence of his criticism— "namely, that in the thirty-seventh verse of the "twenty-third chapter of St. Matthew, 'how "'often *would I'*, ought to be changed to 'how "'often *should I'*." This is another instance of Mr. Gould's *"superficial"* reading. My objection was not to the words, *"I would"*; but to the words, *"I would like"*. Mr. G. W. Eveleth, of

Fort Fairfield, attempts a metaphysical defence
of the expression, "*I would like*"; and says;—"*I*
"*would like* to discover either Dr. Cragin or Mr.
"Moon at attempting to *demonstrate* the con-
"trary"; *i.e.*, that the expression is wrong. I
might reply to Mr. Eveleth, in the words of Butt-
mann, as quoted by the late Sir Edmund W.
Head, Bart., in his excellent little work, '*Shall*
'*and Will*', page 7 : "*Man frage nicht warum—*
"*der Sprachgebrauch lässt sich nur beobachten*".
"The idiom of language admits only of being
"observed; let no man ask 'Why?'" But the
impropriety of the expression, "*I would like*",
admits of demonstration. Mr. Gould informs
us that he intended to express "*choice, option,*
"*will*"; but, *liking* is not under the control of
will. To *do* a thing, is certainly a matter of
"*choice, option, will*"; but to *like* to do it, is a
matter which is not in the power of the *will* to
determine. Hence, the absurdity of the expression.

CRITICISM XXII.

EDWARD S. GOULD.

MR. GOULD tells us that he has re-read '*The* '*Dean's English*'; and he says;—

> "That re-reading has enlightened me on one point. "I find that I, at first, read the book very super- "ficially".

Superficialness appears to be a characteristic feature of Mr. Gould's reading. We have seen evidences of it in much that he has written; and we have now a second confession of it from himself. However, *consciousness* of a bad habit in one's self, is, when expressed, a very hopeful sign of ultimate emancipation from its thraldom; and therefore Mr. Gould must, on this point, have our congratulations. In the meantime, the frequent occurrence of evidences of his super-ficialness is not calculated to give us a very exalted idea of his qualifications for the office of public instructor. Besides, what dependence can be placed on the judgment of a man who at one

time says, '*Good English*', page 135;—"*Mr.*
"*Moon's book is a masterpiece both in its extreme*
"*accuracy of style, and in its criticism; and any*
"*one, after reading it, can see how well deserved is the*
"*commendation it has received*"; and at an other
time says, that it is "*a not very accurately written*
"*book*"? The readers of these criticisms will, I
think, be inclined to smile, not less at this change
in Mr. Gould's opinion, than at his apology for it.

In reference to this somewhat suspicious
change, and by way of explaining it, Mr. Gould
says, of '*The Dean's English*';—

> "It received the almost universal commendation of the
> "British press. The British journals and peri-
> "odicals not only spoke in high terms of Mr.
> "Moon's powers as a critic, but also of his style
> "as a writer of English. Indeed, I do not
> "remember to have seen a single exception to
> "the style of '*The Dean's English*' in any of the
> "British or American notices of the book; and I
> "the more incautiously allowed myself to praise
> "its style in my book, under the misleading of
> "such general approval by the critics—of whom,
> "among others, are '*The Westminster*' and
> "[*London*] '*Quarterly Reviews*'."

I am happy in the belief that the critics, both
English and American, will not feel hurt by this

charge of their having misled the public. They
well understand that, from some men, censure is
more complimentary than praise. Mr. Gould is,
certainly, a very fit person to sit in judgment
upon the critics ! *He* never examined any work
"*superficially*"; and, therefore, he never praised
where he should have censured, nor did he ever
censure where he should have praised. All that
he has done, has been *thorough;* consequently,
his opinion has at all times been decisive and
indisputable !

But let us examine the composition of the
passage which I have quoted. Mr. Gould says;—
"The British journals *and* periodicals". In
reference to periodicals, Mr. Gould objects, in
' *Good English*', page 82, to the application of
the word "*journal*", to any other than a *daily*
paper ; because, as he justly remarks, the derivation of the word limits the meaning to that.
A "*journal*", then, is a publication issued *daily;*
and, of course, a "*periodical*" is a publication
issued *periodically.* But " *daily*" is *periodically;*
therefore a "*journal*" is a "*periodical*"; yet Mr.
Gould says;—"journals *and* periodicals"! How
are we to account for this ? How will *he* account
for it ? Will he again plead "*carelessness*"?

To continue, Mr. Gould says;—" The British
"journals *and* periodicals *not only spoke* in high
"terms of Mr. Moon's powers as a critic, *but*
"*also of* his style as a writer of English". A
schoolboy could tell Mr. Gould that the relative
parts of a sentence should agree with each other;
and that there must be something wrong in the
construction when the words, "*not only*", are
followed by a *verb*, while the corresponding
words, "*but also*", are followed by a *preposition :*
e.g., Mr. Gould says that the periodicals "*not*
"*only spoke*", etc., " *but also of*". He cannot
justify his adoption of this form of expression;
nor can he plead ignorance as an excuse for the
error; for I have repeatedly pointed it out to
him; and he, himself, has censured Dean Alford
and others for committing it. Thus, I read in
' *Good English*', page 100;—" Another blunder,
" of which the instances are innumerable, is the
" misplacing of the word ' *only*'. Indeed, this is
" so common, *so absolutely universal*, [!] one may
" almost say that ' *only*' cannot be found in its
" proper place in any book within the whole
" range of English literature . . . The error
" consists in placing ' *only*' before the verb,
" instead of after it; the grammatical effect of

"which is, to make '*only*' apply to the verb,
"instead of [to] what follows the verb". On
Mr. Gould's own showing, then, his sentence is
incorrect. It ought to have been;—" The
" British journals and *other* periodicals spoke in
" high terms, *not only of* Mr. Moon's powers as a
" critic, *but also of* his style as a writer of
" English ". *Superficialness* and *carelessness*
again, I suppose ?

There are other errors in this paragraph respecting ' *The Dean's English* '. Mr. Gould says;—
" and I the more incautiously allowed myself to
" praise its style in my book, under the mislead-
" ing of such general approval by the critics—of
" whom, among others, are ' *The Westminster* '
" and ' *Quarterly Reviews* '. I did not know
that " *critics* " are " *Reviews* " ; I thought them
to be *reviewers*. Again ; " the critics—*of whom,*
" *among others,* are ", etc. Mr. Gould expressed
a hope that I would " *keep quiet on tautology* ";—
the reason is obvious.

After testifying to the favourable opinion
entertained of ' *The Dean's English* ', Mr. Gould
says, in the next sentence ;—

" " *If however,* the style of the book in question is
" *nevertheless* ", etc.

" *If however, nevertheless* " *!*   I wonder whether
this comes up to Mr. Gould's idea of tautology;
and whether, if it does, he will again plead
" *carelessness* ", as his excuse for it.   He seems
to consider that to be a sufficient apology for any
error; *but, yet, still, however, nevertheless, notwithstanding,* he ought to know that " *carelessness* "
is scarcely less injurious to a man's character as a
professor of literature, than is absolute ignorance
itself.

As an additional evidence of Mr. Gould's
" *carelessness* " and " *very superficial* " reading I
bring forward his assertion that, of a certain
kind of error,—

> " Mr. Moon can find but seven [instances] in Dean
> " Alford's book "—" in the Dean's whole book ".

Yet Mr. Gould must have read, on page xii of
my preface to the edition of ' *The Dean's English* '
from which he quotes, that,—" *I did not extend*
" *my criticisms to his* [*The Dean's*] *recently pub-*
" *lished volume,* ' *The Queen's English* '." My
criticisms are on the Dean's essays in ' *Good*
' *Words* '.   So much for Mr. Gould's " *careful* '
examination of ' *The Dean's English* '.

The following are some of the errors which he

professes to have discovered in the course of his
"*careful*" examination of it.

He condemns the expression :—

> "*Those* whom you think to be most in need of im-
> "provement". And he says;—"In common
> "parlance, and in careless writing, '*those*' is used
> "as the equivalent of '*those persons*', etc. But
> "in the sentences of a philological critic who
> "holds a brother critic responsible for every
> "faulty particle in his sentences, '*those*' by itself
> "is inadmissible."

"A little learning is a dangerous thing". The
word "*those*", by itself, is, unquestionably, inad-
missible in certain sentences; but not in sentences
in which it is followed by a relative pronoun ; as
it is in the sentence which Mr. Gould condemns.
If he will refer to '*Lindley Murray's Grammar*',
Rule xxi, section 10, he may read thus:—"The
"examples which follow are produced to show
"the impropriety of ellipsis in some particular
"cases:—'The land was always possessed,
"'during pleasure, by those intrusted with the
"'command'; it should be, '*those persons* in-
'trusted'; or '*those who* were intrusted'".

Again; Mr. Gould condemns the expression
"*to understand* ", in the following sentence :—

"You will take into consideration the extreme diffi-
"culty we have to understand the contradictory
"instructions we have received."

He suggests that it would have been better to
say ;—" Our extreme difficulty *in understanding*";
but he very cautiously adds, *"if that is what is
"meant"*. Now, that is *not* what was meant ;
and it was for that very reason that I used the
other expression. The difficulty spoken of, was
not one that occurred *in the process* of understanding the contradictory instructions received.
The difficulty occurred *at the outset*, before the
mind had been able, in any degree, to grasp
the meaning of the writer's words. Hence,
the propriety of speaking of our difficulty *" to
"understand "* the contradictory instructions.
Mr. Gould's language would imply that the mind
had made some progress in the task before the difficulty occurred ;—that it was *" in understanding "*
the contradictory instructions. But my meaning
was, what my language plainly expresses, namely,
that the mind had made *no progress whatever*, in
the task, before the difficulty occurred ;—the contradictory instructions were still before it as a
task which it had *" to understand "*.

Mr. Gould objects to my saying that,—

P 2

"The faults of teachers, if suffered to pass unre-
"proved, soon become the teachers of faults."

He says ;—" This is neatly antithetical, but it
" is incorrect in fact. Faults may become *ex-*
" *amples,* but they cannot well be *teachers.* "
Indeed! Why not? Teaching does not necessarily imply the possession of volition on the
part of the teacher. Not only Jesus Christ, (I
say it with all reverence,) but nature also, is "*a*
" *teacher sent from God* ".—" Ask now the beasts,
" and they shall *teach* thee ; . . . . or speak to
" the earth, and it shall *teach* thee ": Job xii,
7—9.

As for the language of the Bible, Mr. Gould
condemns me because, in making a quotation
from it, I adhered to the old spelling, and wrote
the verse '*verbatim et literatim*', and spelt
"*forbade*" without the *e* ! A most grave charge,
certainly ; at least, such Mr. Gould tries
to make it appear ; for he does not tell his
readers, as in honesty he ought to do, that my
spelling of the word was in a literal quotation of
the well known passage in 2 Peter, ii, 16 :—
" The dumb ass speaking with man's voice *forbad*
" the madness of the prophet." But, perhaps
Mr. Gould did not know that the quotation is from

the Bible.　If so; all that I can say is;—"the "greater the disgrace!"

Mr. Gould finds fault likewise with the expressions:—

> "It will be only modest of the Dean"; and, "If you will not think it sacrilegious of me".

He says;—"Might not Mr. Moon as well say "'*off* the Dean'; and, '*off* me'?　The proper "word is *in*".　Again, Mr. Gould, in a vain endeavour to find an error in the language of an other writer, really exposes his own ignorance. He is, evidently, not aware that the expressions are elliptical; and that it is as correct to say;— "It will be only modest [on the part] *of* the "Dean"; as it is to say;—"It will be only modest "*in* [the conduct of] the Dean".

The next objection which Mr. Gould raises, is to my saying—stop; I find that the words which *careful* Mr. Gould puts into inverted commas as a quotation, are nowhere to be found in my book! His objection, however, is to my calling the word "*female*" an "*epithet*".　He says;—

> "Here, as elsewhere, Mr. Moon seems to be ignorant "of the meaning of English words.　He calls "the noun, '*female*', an '*epithet*'.　If he would "take the trouble to consult [the reader will

"observe that, according to Mr. Gould, it is
"wrong for *me* to say, '*the difficulty to under-*
"'*stand*'; but right for *him* to say, "*the trouble*
"'*to consult*"] his dictionary, he would find that
"an *epithet* 'is an *adjective* expressing some
"'quality that is appropriate to a person or
"'thing'; as good, bad, etc. Is it possible that
"Mr. Moon is ignorant of the fact that no part
"of speech other than an *adjective* is an *epithet*"?

I reply that it is not only "*possible*", but
actual; for, what Mr. Gould calls a "*fact*", has
really no foundation in truth. I *have* taken the
"trouble to consult" the very dictionary which
he commends most highly, and which, on that
account, I suppose to be the one which he himself consulted,—superficially, of course, as is
consistent with his practice in such matters. In
that dictionary I read as follows:—"'All adjec-
"'tives', says Crabb, 'are epithets; but *all*
"'*epithets are not adjectives.* Thus, in Virgil's
"'*Pater Æneas* (Father Æneas) the *Pater*
"'(Father) is an epithet, but it is not an adjec-
"'tive'." Thus, the very authority to which
Mr. Gould refers me condemns him!

CRITICISM XXIII.

EDWARD S. GOULD.

Mr. Gould objects to my sentence :—

"Let your meaning be obscure, and *no* grace of diction
"*nor* any music of a well-turned period, will
"make amends to your readers for their being
"liable to misunderstand you."

He would say;—"*Neither* grace of diction, *nor*
"any music", etc.; from which correction (?) I
can draw no other inference than that he believes
it to be wrong to use the negative particle *"nor"*,
except as the co-relative of *"neither"*. Again
I refer him to an authority to which he has
appealed,—G. Brown's *'Grammar of English
'Grammars'*. On page 664, I read :—"Undoubt-
"edly a negative may be repeated in English
"without impropriety, and that *in several differ-
"ent ways;* as, 'There is *no* living, *none*, if
"'Bertram be away'.—*Shakespeare.* 'Great
"'men are *not* always wise, *neither* do the aged
"'[always] understand judgment':—Job xxxii, 9.
"'Will he esteem thy riches? *no, not* gold, *nor* all
"'the forces of strength':—Job xxxiv, 19."

Likewise to the following sentence of mine, Mr. Gould objects :—

"This is enough to show that the schoolmaster is "needed by *other* people *besides* the directors."

Mr. Gould would alter this to, *" other than "*. But, here again, it is *he* who is in error; and he is condemned on this point also, by the authority just quoted.   In a foot note on page 678 of '*The* '*Grammar of English Grammars*', I read;— "After '*else*' and '*other*', the preposition '*besides*' "is sometimes used; and when it recalls an idea "previously suggested, it appears to be as good "as '*than*', or better; as, '*other* words, *besides* "'the preceding, may begin with capitals'." The phrase, *" other ... than "*, is *ex*clusive of those mentioned; whereas, *" other ... besides "*, is *in*-clusive of those mentioned.   No slight difference; and yet, one that has escaped the observation of Mr. Gould.

Another sentence to which he objects is the following :—

"I wished to show, by your own writings, that so far "were you from being competent to teach others "English composition, that you had need your- "self to study its first principles."

Mr. Gould's objection is to the repetition of the word "*that*", not on account of its being somewhat inelegant; but, on account of its being positively incorrect; indeed so very incorrect, that he questions whether anything *could* be worse.   I had previously considered that the sentence would be improved by the omission of one of the "*thats*", and in the English edition of ' *The Dean's English*' it had been altered accordingly. But, that the sentence, as it stands in the early edition from which all Mr. Gould's quotations are made, is not *incorrect*, admits of very simple demonstration.

It will, at once, be conceded that it is correct to make a statement thus :—"*So far* were you "from being competent to teach others English "composition, *that* you had need yourself to "study its first principles"; and no one but Mr. Gould would say that it is incorrect to preface that statement by these words;—"*I* "*wished to show*, by your own writings, *that*——".

Yet Mr. Gould says;—"Could anything be "worse than '*that*'?"   Yes, Mr. Gould; many sentences of your own are decidedly worse; sentences, too, in which the error consists of the misuse, or of the omission, of the identical word

under discussion. On page 60, of Mr. Gould's
work, I read :—" Many writers have a habit of
" omitting '*that*', from what would seem to be
" a propensity to over-neatness of style; or, it
" may be omitted through carelessness. The
" omission makes a sentence both inaccurate
" and inelegant."

Was it "*a propensity to over-neatness of style*"
which induced Mr. Gould, four times in one
letter to '*The Round Table*', to omit the word
"*that*", where its presence was needed; or is the
omission but another evidence of his "*careless-*
"*ness* "?

Compare his remarks on this subject with his
practice in the following sentences :—

> "I hope [that] he is not so far lost ".
> "Mr. Moon says [that] '*a deal* of argument is
> " ' wrong '."
> "I think [that] Mr. Moon ought to know ".
> "Mr. Moon says [that] my errors are *so* droll ".

Mr. Gould objects to my speaking of

> "the childish prattle of our little ones ";

and he says ;—" Mr. Moon ! could you not say,
" 'the prattle of children '?" Certainly, Mr.
Gould, I could; but I greatly prefer the tender-

ness of the former expression, to the comparative unlovingness of the latter.

Mr. Gould, knowing that I censured Dean Alford for confusedly mixing the tenses of verbs, exults in what he believes to be the discovery of a confusion of tenses in a paragraph of mine. He says;—" Mr. Moon knows that Dean Alford " occasionally mixes the past and present tenses; " and that the mixture is a fault.   Yet Mr. Moon "gives us, on page 106, this:— [Perhaps Mr. Gould will pardon me if I add to his quotation certain words which he chose to omit.]

> " It was not until I had long and hopelessly pondered
> "over your sentence, that I discovered what it
> "*was* you intended to say, and what *was* the
> "reason of my not instantly catching your mean-
> "ing.   I find that the first clause in your
> " sentence *is* inverted, and that the punctuation
> "necessary to make the inversion *is* incorrect, or
> " rather *is* altogether omitted ".

Here, again, it is Mr. Gould who is in error. The two sentences are perfectly distinct, and each is correct.   The first *relates to the past*—to what I "discover*ed*", to what was "intend*ed*".   The other sentence *relates to the present*—to what " I *find*", namely, that the clause " *is* inverted ", and that the punctuation *is* incorrect ", etc.   My condemnation of the Dean, was for his confusion of tenses in *a sentence;* not for his change of tense in *a paragraph.*

I really feel that I ought to apologize to my readers for noticing some of Mr. Gould's remarks. They are simply puerile, and do not deserve so much as a passing notice, except for the purpose of showing how unwisely even an educated man may be tempted to write, when for a time his mind is bent upon detracting from the merit of an opponent.

Further; Mr. Gould says;—"On page 94, he "[Mr. Moon] assumes to amend one of the "Dean's sentences, and says that his amend-"ment 'is correct'. The amendment is in these "words:—

"'If with your inferiors, speak not more coarsely "'than *usual*'.

"The Dean's sentence is, 'Speak no *coarser* "'than usual": and it was very well for Mr. "Moon to object to *one* adjective and to put an "adverb in its place; but it seems strange, that "while his attention was directed to adverbs and "adjectives, he could overlook another adjective "in the same line which requires the same

" change ! *Usual* is an adjective, not an adverb.
" And when Mr. Moon, by way of correcting the
" Dean's line, changes *coarser* and leaves *usual*
" unchanged, he commits the same blunder as
" [that which] he has just condemned in the Dean.
" And he intrenches himself in his own blunder
" by the affirmation that the line, as *amended,*
" ' is correct '. Whether it is correct or not, is
" shown by supplying the omitted words of the
" ellipsis :—' Speak not more coarsely than [you]
" ' usual [do] '! "

That is all very good in its way, Mr. Gould ;
but when we find an ellipsis in a writer's sentence,
it behoves us not to be dogmatical as to what
words he has omitted; nor ought we to accuse
him of inaccuracy because his sentence, *according
to our filling up of it,* is ungrammatical; when
there is an other way of filling it up; and when,
according to *that* filling up of it, the language will
be found to be correct. It is not improbable that
the Dean meant :—" Speak not more coarsely than
" [is] usual"; or, " Speak not more coarsely than
" [it is] usual [for you to speak.] " *It was therefore only just toward him, to leave unaltered the last
word of his sentence.*

However, if Mr. Gould is particularly anxious

to find a sentence in which a verb is qualified by
both an adverb and an adjective, he need not go
very far for it. On page 125, of his own work,
there is the following sentence :—

> " ' As closely as possible' means as *closely* as possible,
> " and no *closer* ".

The words refer to the rule that the parts of a
sentence which are "*connected* in meaning should
" be *connected* in position *as closely as possible* ".
Therefore, Mr. Gould's expression is really this:—
" [*Connected*] 'as closely as possible' means, [con-
"nected] *as closely as possible, and* [connected]
"*no closer*"!   Look at home, Mr. Gould!   Look
at home!

When Mr. Gould meets with what to him is a
difficulty, instead of acknowledging in humility
that at present he is not equal to its solution, he
has a method of his own of dealing with it,
which is deserving of attention here.   It is
evident that, confidently as he speaks concerning the necessity for our putting nouns into
the possessive case when they are followed by
present participles, he has some misgivings
respecting the universal application of the rule ;
otherwise, it seems improbable that he would

resort to the practice of misquoting an opponent's words, lest, in their natural order, they should prove to be irreconcilable with a certain favourite theory.

Mr. Gould gives what he calls "*a complete* "*list*" of the instances in which, in ' *The Dean's* '*English*', I have used a noun before a present participle, without putting the noun into the possessive case. I have spoken of this matter in Criticism XIX; and I revert to it, merely to notice Mr. Gould's additional remarks. It will rather surprise my readers to be told that, notwithstanding Mr. Gould's assertion, he has *not* really given us "*a complete list*" of the instances mentioned.

Mr. Gould may again plead "*carelessness*"; or, he may tell us that his second reading of ' *The* '*Dean's English*' was, like the first, "*very super-* "*ficial*"; but it is rather suspicious, that what he has omitted from his "*complete list*", happens to be a part of one of those difficult sentences which it is more than probable he was at a loss how to treat according to the rule laid down by him.

Why, from his "*complete list*," did he leave out part of the sentence which he pretended

to quote from page 93? His quotation is
as follows :—" *Owing to the term being capable* ".
But my sentence is :—

> " Owing to the term '*no more*' being capable of mean-
> "ing", etc.

I suppose that he would not like to write,
either ;—" Owing to the term'*s* 'no more' being
capable of meaning ", etc. ; or, " Owing to the
term 'no more'*s* ' being capable of meaning ",
etc.; and therefore—but it was merely " *careless-*
"*ness* ", of course—he gave in his " *complete list* ",
a garbled quotation of the sentence !

Mr. Gould appears to be not only an admirer
of Dean Alford, but also an imitator of him ;
and, as is usual with persons who are not remarkable for originality, he imitates that which,
in his model, is least worthy of imitation. The
Dean is fond of a joke ; and, of course, Mr.
Gould, also, must for once try to be witty; so
he writes thus ; first pretending to quote from
page vii of ' *The Dean's English* ' :—

> " 'The Dean has altered *and* struck out not fewer
> "'than eight-and-twenty passages which I had
> "' condemned as faulty.' "

Mr. Gould says;—"That is as thoroughly "*Irish* as anything in '*The Queen's English*'. If "the passages were *struck out* how could they be "*altered*—since striking them out made an end "of them? To be sure, they might have been "altered and afterward stricken out [*struck out;*] * "but, in that case, how could Mr. Moon *know* "anything of the alteration? I would advise "him to alter *or* strike out *his own* sentence. The "real state of the case is shown on pages 126— "139: *twenty* passages are '*altered*' and *eight* "are '*struck out*'."

No doubt, Mr. Gould wished the readers of '*The Round Table*' to consider his criticism as very witty. They will, however, probably give it another name when they know that the joke is at the sacrifice of *truth!* I do *not* say;—"The "Dean has altered and struck out not fewer than "eight-and-twenty passages". My words are;— "The Dean has altered and struck out, *altogether* "not fewer than eight-and-twenty passages".

Why did Mr. Gould omit, from his quotation

---

* "When the verb has different forms, that form should be adopted which is the most consistent with present and reputable usage in the style employed". We ought not to say;—'The 'clock hath *stricken*'".—'*Grammar of English Grammars*', *p.* 577.

of my sentence, the one word which proves the falseness of his statement?

Why, too, did he speak of me as one "*who,* "*'with no uncertain sound', assumes infallibility* "*for his own English*"; when he was well aware that, in Criticism XVIII, I had said;—"*I no* "*more lay claim to infallibility than I do to omni-* "*science*"?

Moreover, Mr. Gould knew that, in a note courteously censuring him for his discourteous language, the editor of '*The Round Table*' had closed the controversy between us, at least as regards the insertion of any more of it in the columns of '*The Round Table*', and that it was only as a special favour that Mr. Gould's request for the insertion of an other letter from him was granted. He ought, therefore, like an honourable man, to have shrunk with especial care from making any statement which bore the semblance of an untruth, seeing that I was debarred the privilege of replying to it.

Honest criticism I value most highly. A witty remark, or a smart repartee, I can always appreciate. But when a writer has recourse to the meanest of all questionable practices in order to give zest to his criticisms and point to his otherwise feeble wit, I tell him plainly, that his criticisms and his witticisms alike are deserving of contempt.

Shall I part thus with my opponent? No! rather let me, in very charity towards him, do violence even to my own judgment in the matter, and ascribe his misstatements, as well as his errors, to "*carelessness*" and "*very superficial*" reading; and tell him that, notwithstanding all, I have derived much amusement from his writings, as well as some instruction.

THE END.